Ravan's Trial

SUNDAR NATHAN

INDIA • SINGAPORE • MALAYSIA

ISBN 979-8-88783-550-1

Dedicated to the Intuitive Feeler, the Dreamer, the Joyful Storyteller who lives within each of us.

Khusgul Lake
Steppe
Khargas Lake
Great Narakan Desert
IKSHURA OCEAN
N
W
E
S

NARAKA
Physical Map

Contents

Acknowledgements

First and foremost, I want to thank Lord Shiva for giving me the strength and courage to start my writing journey and endure significant challenges on the journey. Om Namo Bhagavate Rudraayaa!

I want to thank Jesse Tate for his intense coaching, editing, and support throughout my journey with *The Naraka Cycle*. You are a brilliant, kind, and inspirational human being. I am so privileged to know you and to have had the opportunity to work with you on this project.

Kaushie Adiseshan and Anand Rajaraman, I vividly remember reading the final chapter of the trilogy, *The Naraka Cycle*, to you in your living room and the encouragement you gave me to continue. Thank you for your love and support all through this journey.

Nilesh Parate, my man, words cannot express my gratitude for your friendship, encouragement, and support. You and Joycie have been pillars of support.

Corey Sommers, this novel would not be what it is without your 'whippleage.' My brother from another mother, your incredible attention to detail and mastery of the English language are unparalleled. Thank you for helping me uncover issues and guiding me with fixing them.

Amma (Saroja Viswanathan), thank you for being my first beta reader and for extensive feedback. I love you and appreciate your support.

Subhakka (Subha Barry), thank you for the guidance, introductions, and encouragement, as always!

Sujatha Suresh, thank you for your marketing insights and connecting me with the right people.

Chikni Pati (Namagiri Ammal) and Vasu Mama (S. Vasudevan), thank you for your stories!

Anna Lisitsa, your friendship and affection mean a great deal to me. Murali Nair, my brother, I got it done!! Your affection is boundless.

Thank you.

Anushka Shankar, your help with research, helping me with the story grid, project management, shlokas, languages, glossary, and so much more, was invaluable. Your perspectives on Surpanakha and Vaasuki as young women were super helpful. Thank you from the bottom of my heart.

Logan Beaton, your hard work and dedication as project manager, visual creator, and producer were vital. Thank you.

Chris Capelle, thank you for your tremendous support.

Rajvardhan Kadam and Harshvardhan Kadam, you guys are geniuses. The cover illustrations, final maps, and book layout are brilliant. I am truly humbled to have had the opportunity to work with you both.

Sotirios Tzavelas and Achilleas Papoutsopoulos, your illustrations and initial maps helped me visualize the geography of Naraka!

Jena Starkes, you've created a beautiful website! Thank you so much.

Lauren Brooks, thank you for the first round of editing, and for giving me the detailed feedback I needed to improve the novel substantially.

To my Kung Fu SiHings, and now SiFus, Stephen Chew and Onassis Parungao, your coaching and support helped me keep my mind and body healthy as I fought through the challenges with outlining, writing, editing, and the many, many revisions of this novel.

Tanvi Naren, Vikram Naren, Saadhana Ramani and Ishaan Parate, I want to thank you so much for the art ideas, research assistance, and

Viswanathan Anand, Jeetendra Vummidi, Vinod Ethirajan, Ram Bhatt, Ravi Ivaturi, and Deepak Shanker, my Don Bosco brothers, I want to thank you sincerely for your love and encouragement.

Ganesh Ranganathan, without the 'vollaral' we share and your wonderful support, I'm not sure I would have finished the journey. Thank you.

Jay Barry, your encouragement and love mean the world to me. Arvind Subramaniam, Nandini Ramesh, Adam and Caroline Clark, Shanker Kuttath and Divya Shanker, Lynn and Barbara White, Rachael Burns, Jodi Jackson, Uddhav Joshi, Shish Mukherjee, and Samyukta.

Suresh—my dear Austin family—you were such important catalysts on many occasions. This novel would not have been possible without your love, and support.

Shankar Raghavan, Ramani Krishnan, D. Sivakumar, Vijaya Mohan, Ganesh Ranganathan, thank you from the bottom of my heart.

Last but not least, my dear *pattu paapu*, Rudra Pratap Singh, loving Rocky Rockefeller, and beloved Orry Oliver, you remain my pillars of encouragement and strength. Woof woof!

Preface

The Puranas and the great Indian epics are rich with incredible life lessons and intriguing characters. Perhaps the greatest blessing of my childhood growing up in India was hearing wonderful stories and myths from my *paati* and *amma,* snippets of lore derived from these histories, mythologies, and epics. Thus began my seven-year journey to fashion the first instalment of *The Naraka Cycle: Ravan's Trial.*

While the inspiration for the characters and their lineages is sourced from the great Indian epics, readers may find their particular trials and tribulations familiar and somewhat modern. My goal is to create a connective tissue between personal, modern struggles and mythological lore, all supported by a fast-moving, riveting, supernatural fantasy saga.

While characters such as Ravan or Indra may be familiar to some of you, I've challenged the conventional wisdom of some of their origin stories in ways readers might find interesting and perhaps even audacious. I invite readers to explore and consider these twists with an open mind and remember that we all evolve and grow in different ways as we take our own journeys through life to seek our true destinies.

Prologue

On Swarga, Indra was in fine, high humour. The banquet celebrating mainland Swargan unification—the feast to cement his rule—was going as beautifully as he could have ever desired. The abundance of his table sated the hunger in Indra's belly. The hunger of his ears was filled with the sweetness of the melodies woven by his *gandharvan* musicians. The hunger in his eyes was made ravenous by the gyrations of the most beautiful courtesans of all the known realms, his *apsaras*.

"Interesting, is it not?" Indra mused idly, turning to the High Lord of Death, Yama, who sat beside him. "The hunger in the eyes is the only hunger which, when met, only further grows to find itself insatiable."

"Ahh?" Yama's left eyebrow arched theatrically. "Do enlighten us, good Indra." Around the table, the others turned to listen—Agni, Dhanvantri, Vayu. The High Devan Lords of the various kingdoms of Swarga. *My former enemies, my current allies. But never my friends. I brought them to their knees through Saama, Daana, Bheda, or Danda. Alliance, Gifts, Trickery, or All-Out War.*

A conqueror could not be friends with the conquered. *I will use them. Use their strength when needed. But always, they will seek to chip away at the legs of my throne, to topple it from under me.*

His sister and general, Jayanti Prabalha, ignored Yama, rolling her almond eyes and returning to her discussion with Agni, High Lord of Fire. They were still debating how to respond to the Rakshasan pirates of Naraka, a realm separated from Swarga by the icy Kshirada Sea.

Coolly—deliberately—Indra met the eyes of his four high lords, allowing himself the slightest edge of a smile. *Yama is the mischievous one, fomenting doubt among the others. He engages in constant, petty power posturing. I need to keep an eye on him.*

That night, though, Indra felt as strong as an entire brood of Swargan *garudas*, golden eagles. *And twice as fierce.* He met Yama's goad with a careless grin. "Hunger," he repeated to the table. "The hunger of the eyes is the only hunger which, when met, further grows to find itself insatiable." The emperor motioned down towards the inner court, where the apsara women wove their lithe, enchanting dance. Their bodies glistened, oily smooth, beneath the flicker of the open flames that lit the vast hall. "We see a single almond eye revealed from behind a bejewelled veil. And think a mere glimpse of the other would satisfy us. But then, the other eye appears. Then, we see the curve of a nose. Just the face, we think, and then our eyes will be content."

Agni and Dhanvantri nodded. Yama grinned. Vayu was impassive. Indra smiled, his fair hair gleaming in the lights of the hall. *While their lust for power will persist, they can hardly resist what I offer them. Luxury and abundance, yes, but also the respite needed to enjoy it.*

A stop to endless war. Peace across all of Swarga.

His dream had hardened him, and forced him to embrace their games. But the dream was swiftly becoming a reality. *Once I subdue that vijaata, Varuna, I will rule all of Swarga.*

The High Devan Lords waited, their bellies satiated, their tongues loosened by his best wine. Indra took a deep draught of *sura* wine, and then continued. "A bit more, we think. The throat perhaps, and the baring of a shoulder." He traced the figure of a woman in the air. "A shoulder. A leg. A breast. Each fails to suffice. They only spark hunger for the next—to go further." He gestured at the gyrating apsaras once again. The High Lords nodded and smiled, their attention torn between their conqueror and the bewitching bodies in the firelight.

From all corners of Swarga, the apsaras came to be trained in the mastery of their art—the art of the assassin seductress. To be unleashed by their master on his unsuspecting rivals.

"The only hunger that gives rise directly to another," Indra finished, "is the hunger for touch, for conquest."

Yama clicked his tongue loudly, destroying the moment. "Not for me," he said, shaking his head with a grin. "For me, that's every sort of hunger." He touched his ears. "I hear a little maiden sing? I come closer." He tapped his nose. "I smell an apsara's devilish perfume? I seek it out." He widened his eyes. "I see her curves?" He opened his mouth. "And when I taste her lips. . . "

Yama gestured towards an especially beautiful apsara with a leer. "I only ever want more. Not just a tender maiden. A proud warrior. A stupid farmer, laughing in his ignorance, By Brahma's heads, a flower. I want to close in, to touch, to feel." He smiled, dropping a strangely wizened hand to caress an exquisite gold-plated quillon dagger at his hip.

"To kill," Indra nodded, unimpressed. "We know, Yama. You're the servant of Kaala, of Death himself. So you've been reminding us for centuries."

"I am Kaala's *chief!*" Yama flared, head tilting to one side, lips parting in a grin he meant to be unnerving. Indra merely found it shallow. Formless. A silhouette of power already snatched away.

Indra had faced death in many forms, and every time, emerged the stronger. He no longer feared its embrace.

"You speak too much, Yama," Jayanti Prabalha, 'the Strong One' turned at last with a lazy smile, plucking a grape from Yama's plate and popping it into her luscious, mouth. "You should eat, so you have the strength to go forth on all those promised conquests."

Indra chuckled at Yama's comical expression. The tension at the table receded as Jayanti tactfully led the High Lords into a good-natured argument as to who could muster the better army and navy.

My precious Jayanti. She leads my forces with strategy and ferocity. A season for allies, a season for finesse, a season for trickery, and a season for outright war. Indra and Jayanti had campaigned together for centuries.

But she isn't prepared for what's to come, he thought coldly. *She fails to see I've outgrown her. She's blinded by her affection and allegiance to me.*

Indra resolved to nurture neither. In his experience, the survival of only the fittest under him was most efficient. He had just a few more lands to bring to heel, praise Brahma. One language, one faith, one God, one peace—Indra's peace—to last a yuga. *A million years. A few more battles, a few more seeds of greed and power-lust to sow among the weak-willed, and I will prevail, by Brahma.*

Yes. Yama is a bother, but I have him well in hand. Death is ever greedy. Ever showy. But in the end, it is mere noise. So much vanity. My father, Brahma, breathes new life.

Idly, Indra turned away, basking for a moment in the splendour of his hall. Rich velvet tapestries adorned the walls, and the vaulted ceiling was decorated with frescoes of Brahma, the God of Creation. His gaze landed once more on his striking apsaras. The most beautiful women of all the lands the apsaras were, sweet and full but supple and strong, not an ounce of their bodies wasted. Each of them was as cunning as any general, as elegant and deadly as a concealed quillon dagger.

The Throne Room was his pride and joy, the crowning jewel of his new palace in Amaravati, the capital of Indrapura. He'd wanted it to be the grandest in all the realms, the most beautiful in recorded history. Five-sided, a wall for each Narakan kingdom he had conquered, four of them adorned with the art and history of its people. The fifth lay unadorned. *I will bring the Kinnaran bastards on Naraka to heel soon enough.* Carvings of ancient Devan heroes and ferocious battles with the five Narakan kingdoms marched along the cornices, etched in bas-relief. Five pillars fronted each wall in an outer circle and five slimmer designs as they neared the hall's centre. Statues of lissom apsaras danced and twisted at the base of each column, fluid and almost lifelike. *Brahma could have them dancing with their flesh-and-blood counterparts with a single breath.*

They'd been carved by his Vidyadharan artisans, of course. The finest stone workers in all the realms. *Pity I can't take over their mountain kingdoms this year,* Indra brooded. His forces were still too scattered, stretched too thin.

A few more seasons, he consoled himself. *Then, I'll move on from the jungles and the plains to the mountains, the desert, the islands, and the steppe, whatever they may hold. For now, I have to make do with three Devan forts and complete control over central Naraka.* Even that would have been a stretch if it hadn't been for the Narakans' penchant for squabbling amongst themselves like spoiled children.

"As long as the taxes pour in," he had told his mentor and chief priest Brihaspati, "I don't care if they tear each other to pieces. *A few more years, a handful of decisive battles, and all of Naraka will be mine.*

Yes. Indra hummed a contented raga, a sweet melody, as he scanned the room, enjoying the sight of his guests, many of whom now cavorted with the apsaras. *This is how it should be. Delectable food, rare sura wine, beautiful women. All shared in Swargan brotherhood.*

One of the new girls hovered at his elbow, waiting as he finished a dish of roast quail. The moment he'd picked the last bone clean, the nimble *Asuran* whisked the plate away. Another scrambled forward with wine and the latest epicurean novelty—grilled peacock from Bhooloka. *The epitome of service. One day—if Brahma smiles—all of Swarga will live like this.*

"Not that, girl!" He waved a hand, flaxen hair and gold rings glittering in the firelight. "Something sweet. I've had enough meat." He didn't scold her, of course. The quail remained his favourite, and all the servants knew that.

"You're new," he observed, admiring her body as she bent to fill his bejewelled silver cup.

"Yes, Your Majesty," she muttered softly. Her gaze remained fixed on the pitcher in her hands.

"Well, speak up! How long have you been at the palace?" he asked, frowning. *Are they so frightened of me that they don't dare give a proper answer? I'm not a monster.*

"Two weeks, Your Majesty," she stammered.

"By Kaala's halls, would you *look* at me while we're speaking?" the emperor hissed, snatching at the fringe of her bodice. "What do they teach you lot down there?"

"They. . . " she gasped, looking terrified. Her eyes darted up to his forehead, flicked down across his eyes, and slipped away. "They teach us not to look," she whispered, head down. "Not to speak. They teach us you're not to be. . . to be. . . "

"What rubbish!" he cursed. "Even when *spoken* to? Do they discourage common manners?"

"Forgive me if I've displeased you. They said. . . " She trembled.

"Fear. . . " He groaned and slapped his forehead, cursing under his breath. "Is this what they teach you? By Brahma, you're supposed to see the *beauty* of this place. Perhaps they'd be well advised to remember *they* are. . . " *Fools.*

"Disappointing, girl," Indra muttered. "Can you not enjoy the luxury of this place? The opulence?"

"Majesty." Her gaze slid down to a spot between her feet. "This place is beautiful. I have seen nothing like it."

"But you miss home," he muttered. "You are afraid. You *will* learn to love this place, I swear it." *Swarga will be a beacon for all the known realms, unmatched in beauty and power.* "Tell me about home, girl. What is the most beautiful place you have seen down in Naraka, in your Nagan wilder village?"

She flinched. "*Wilder* village?" she echoed. A flicker of defiance, masking disgust. "I am no *wilder,* Majesty." She practically spat the word out. "I am a *cityer* from Bhagavassi, of pure Nagan blood."

"Ahh." Indra sighed with a smile. *I should probably address this rather abrupt flare of defiance, however slight. Ahh well. Damn them all to the pyres along the great river Sandhyaa.* "Off with you, girl." He waved a hand dismissively. "Cool off. No more work tonight. If anyone tries to make you, send them to me."

As she struggled to bow and then scurried off, he tried to imagine her transforming. Shedding her skin, stretching herself out of it, and lengthening into a massive, scaled serpent, long as two banquet tables put together.

It was a thought to give any conscious creature pause. Indra had seen it hundreds of times, but still, a Naga transforming was like nothing in the known realms. *Should we even keep Nagas with all the other servants?* They were by far the most contentious and dangerous, given their shape-shifting abilities. *We put spell-bands around their throats, mantra-wards to keep them from shifting, but still. . .*

He smiled thinly. She'd proven one thing: even in chains, deep-seated Narakan hatreds did not vanish.

He returned his attention to his chalice with a sigh, fingers tracing the gems encrusting its beaten silver rim.

"Not right now." He waved Jayanti away as she leaned in to speak with him, lips bright and deadly. "Go weave your charms among the High Lords."

Indra took a long draught, abruptly wishing that he were in the company of his concubines instead of the motley crowd that surrounded him. His mood had turned distinctly sour.

* * *

"I'm telling you he *said* it!" Namissa spat angrily at her overseer, a stodgy, corpulent, fair-haired Devan blocking her path and waving his hands in the doorway of the kitchens. *He's trying to block me from getting by him, the mad Deva. Kenuaa!*

"I don't care what you *say* he said," the overseer sneered, a cloud of flour descending from his flailing arms. "You're too distraught to serve anyone, but you can cut up bread or load the carts or—"

"*Thegêmā dasyu!* You, slave!" Tum Vura, first steward of Guntur, of Indra's palace household came marching up, uniform perfect as always.

Namissa and the fat Devan overseer cowered. The girl had never spoken directly with the woman. Tum Vura was famously tyrannical.

"Namissa, is it?"

"Y—yes?" *She knows my name?*

"What's going on, Namissa?"

"His Grace, *Chakravarthi* Indra has said I may be excused for the night," Namissa stammered. "He said I was distraught, unfit to serve. He said I might—"

"Is this true?" Tum Vura turned to the obese overseer.

"I. . . I have no idea, First Steward," he shrugged. "But it sounds as likely as a bloody Rakshasan wench being crowned queen of—"

"She brought you a message from our emperor—may He live forever—and you didn't even *verify* it before dismissing it outright?"

"But Mistress Tum Vura," he protested. "Imagine! She's—"

"Our servants often carry messages from Devan lords, do they not?"

"They do, Tum Vura, but—"

"And we follow the orders in those messages without question, do we not?"

"We do, but—"

"And every servant in this palace has been trained to tell the truth upon pain of death?"

"They have, and—"

"Then, you're expected to *believe* her," the steward snapped, brushing him aside. The Deva sidestepped with a gulp and watched as the steward motioned Namissa on.

"I'll see to him later," the woman promised briskly as the overseer retreated with a scowl into the bustle of the kitchens.

"For now, though, please tell me what's happened to make you so distraught."

"It was nothing, mistress..." Namissa muttered, averting her gaze. "I just. . . got flustered."

"New here, aren't you?" the woman exclaimed.

"That's right, ma'am."

"Well, let me tell you something, Namissa," the steward said, taking her hand and forcing her to a stop. They faced each other in the dimly lit hallway. "I'm the first steward. I need to keep the royal household running smoothly *every* hour of *every* day. That is my burden. What is the first rule of serving?"

"We are spokes in the wheel that keeps the palace moving," Namissa quoted stiffly. "But we are *not* alive when we serve the palace. Off duty, we are alive. On duty, we are the hand that pours the wine, the voice that announces the arrival of guests, the broom that sweeps the dirt." *We are spokes in a wheel and nothing more.* Nagas did not understand the concept of slavery—but even if they had, they would not have treated slaves as dregs of the realm. Instead, her people would have recognized even a slave's place in the great harmony of their serpent God, Vritra.

"Right." Tum Vura nodded. "So if a *single* piece is out of place, the palace falters. It's my duty to ensure that doesn't happen. Now do you see why you must answer my question?"

Namissa trembled.

"Come, child. Or should I ask the chakravarthi, the emperor himself?"

At first, Namissa recounted only a shadow of the exchange. When the first steward pressed, she sighed and gave her full account.

"I see." It was difficult to tell, but Namissa thought the steward smiled in the darkness. She bristled in anticipation of the woman's wrath. She'd take it, but not kindly. *Somewhere in this hell, I need a touch of pride. A banner to raise and cling to in the eye of the storm. If it can't be in front of Indra, it will damn well be in front of the other servants.*

"I did wrong. I shouldn't have looked the chakravarthi in the eyes—but he told me to look up! And, when he said I was a wilder, perhaps I should have just stayed quiet, but—"

"I'd like to tell you something, Namissa."

It's my guess you intend to, regardless. "What?"

"Hey kache thenunåma, ā Naga ki ri."

Namissa flinched. "What?" she hissed hoarsely. "*What* did you say?" *She is one of us.* Tum Vura, first steward of the palace, was a *Naga*. "You're. . . "

"Yes." The older woman nodded proudly, eyes glimmering in the darkness. "I was brought here as a little girl, captured decades ago and raised here, trained by the very finest of our emperor's—"

"I hate it here!" Namissa burst out. "I *hate* this freezing place. It stinks. The rain is cold; everything is cold! I feel naked in the open plains! And the wind! The wind across the grass. By the Sun Elemental that warms us every morning, the wind and rain freeze me to my bones!" *Wind and rain are to refresh, to bring life. To kiss with coolness the steamy chaos of the jungle. They aren't meant to freeze an already darkened land.*

The first steward watched in silence. She had no mantra-ward around her neck.

"But most of all," Namissa hissed, "I hate *him*. Not just his questions. His eyes! Vritra's tomb, his eyes!" *They are green like life, fierce like fire, and they draw me in. They are terrifying. I felt naked under his gaze.* "He *looks* at me, Tum Vura. Really *looks*." *That isn't normal.*

The others never look—Jayanti and Agni and the dark-haired Yama. No one ever sees a servant—no one, except Indra, the most powerful and terrifying of them all.

"It's as if he wants me to *like* him!" she shuddered. "As if he thinks this place is pure, as if—"

The Naga girl's head rocked back from the steward's slap. A slap so hard she heard the sinews in her neck crack. Spots danced before her eyes, and she staggered against the wall with a gasp.

"Two things." Like lightning, the steward had transformed, taking the form of a giant serpent and wrapping Namissa in her coils.

She's a Naga!

TumVura was a constrictor Naga, lacking in venom but thick as the trunk of a tree. A strong Rakshasa might hack at those scales with an axe and fail to cut cleanly through with a dozen blows.

And she was without a mantra-ward around her throat. Her voice was cold as ice. "The first. You will *never* speak of His Majesty, or of this noble land, in such a vile way again. You will not so much as *think* sour thoughts about the Devas, our masters. You will return to your dormitory for the night, and you will reflect on what you have done. And when you rise tomorrow, you will rise a new creation. You will serve this kingdom until you die, and you will do so cheerfully."

The coils moved, pressing against Namissa's body. With every exhalation, they tightened, cutting off circulation and leaving the Naga girl gasping desperately for air. The hallway blurred around her, and the steward's words echoed as if from a great distance. "The second. Know that I would die for His Majesty. That I would take a thousand arrows for him. That I would harvest a thousand Nagan skins if he asked me to. I am a Naga, true. But I am *of* Swarga now. I *belong* to him. I believe in his vision, Namissa, and some day, you will, too."

Then, they were at eye level again. The steward stood before her a woman, and Namissa found that she could finally breathe.

"Namissa of Naraka," Tum Vura whispered as Namissa gasped for breath. "This is what comes to those who refuse to lay down their foolishness. This is what comes to those who let anger and hatred blind them. I pray you will be born again to Swarga one day. But until that day. . . " smiling ever so sweetly, she patted the magical spell-ward around Namissa's neck. "I'll be watching, and you'll keep this on."

* * *

Namissa crouched in the darkness, moonlight breaking through the clouds to illuminate the clearing just before her. She was in the palace gardens, as far from the servants' quarters as she could risk without her mistress, Talaani, growing suspicious.

She didn't have long. She'd slipped out under the pretext of needing to use the privy. She already had an excuse prepared if she were caught. A wine stain on her skirts, a tear at the bodice of her dress, and her hair tousled about her face. The palace swarmed with Swargan revellers, drunk on Indra's pompous 'generosity.' As with all political gatherings on Swarga, men were everywhere—bearded, wheezing lords and warriors from the far reaches of Swarga, whose wives were far too delicate for such boisterous affairs.

Barbarians. Namissa sniffed in disdain. Where she came from in Nagapura, women were dominant. They stood or slithered with spines, and their men fought fang and coil alongside their warrior wives.

Still, tonight she was delighted for the chauvinistic ways of the Devas of Swarga. *Who knows what the Devan men might do?* Lurching about as they were in a raucous, lust-filled daze, searching for anything that moved and was warmer than a rat three hours old.

Excuse well prepared, Namissa had hurried down the servants' corridor out into the palace lawns, slipped behind the rhododendron hedges, and stolen off to the clearing in the garden.

It was one of her favourites. Lord Poosha and his latest consort favoured it for its 'tranquillity'—another way of saying it guaranteed that the general public wouldn't see their less-than-proper conduct—and Namissa had been recognized as a tight-lipped and quick-footed servant, ideal for carting various wines and pastries to the area without being spotted. *As I helped that maaseru, that jackal, with his whore, I started to love this little clearing.*

Namissa flushed at the memories, feeling a familiar tingle through her core. She'd been a maiden—hardly more than a child—when the Devas had kidnapped her. She'd known the stories, of course, but that was all—just stories. Her Nagan friends, Fenitraa and Staashii, were always bragging about their latest conquest of boys in their quarter of the Nagan capital, Bhagavassi.

She didn't think she'd witness such things within her very first weeks on Swarga. It was–

No. Not now. Hissing in irritation until the tingling warmth subsided, Namissa forced herself to return to the present.

To justice. The sacrificial ring was ready. Four diyas were set out on either side, two each for Naraka and Swarga. The circle around her held five diyas. *One for each of the Narakan races. Naga. Kinnara. Rakshasa. Vidyadhara. Asura.*

The Nagan and Kinnaran diyas were the largest, signifying their sanctity as the purest of races. The Wildest Ones, the ones who lived in harmony with nature. Traditionally, the ritual used torches, but she'd only been able to smuggle the small lamps out of the servants' quarters.

She hoped her God would still hear her prayers.

She first made a *murti* of her five-headed Nagan God, Vritra, using the sacred red soil of Ishvaan that she had stolen from the kitchens. Then, placing the image in the middle of the sacrificial ring, she gave it a holy bath with water that a Nagan female priestess had blessed. Vritra's tiny murti was then bathed with milk and decorated with vermilion, turmeric paste, and fragrant jasmine.

As she uttered the sacred mantras of the Nagas, she wept. . .

ब्रह्म लोके च ये सर्पाः वृत्रनागाः पुरोगमाः|
नमोऽस्तु तेभ्यः सुप्रीताः प्रसन्नाः सन्तु मे सदा ||

(Even in the land of Brahma, Vritra Naga leads these serpents; I salute them, let them be pleased with me for all time.)

प्रलये चैव ये सर्पाः नरक प्रमुखाश्चये।
नमोऽस्तु तेभ्यः सुप्रीताः प्रसन्नाः सन्तु मे सदा॥

(Even at the time of the great dissolution, these serpents were dominant over Naraka; I salute them, let them be pleased with me for all time.)

And then, Namissa cried out in the darkness, "Oh Supreme Vritra, when will you send the armies of Naraka to rescue us?"

NORTHERN RAKSHASA ISLANDS
ERUDO
RAKSHU
Khusgul Lake
STEPPE KINNARAS
Khargas Lake
DESERT KINNARAS
MARUT CASTLE
IKSHURA OCEAN
Naga Wilder Villages
RATNAPUR
AGNI CASTLE
Naga Wilder Villages
Rakshasa Villages
Rakshasa Villages
Rakshasa Villages
Rakshasa Villages
SUNDARA STRAITS
RAKSHARATTHA
SOUTHERN RAKSHASA ISLANDS
PUHAR

NARAKA
Political Map

Chapter 1

The Way of Perfection

Day One

Ravan felt the jungle waiting. He sensed it, deep and vast and silent, breathing with a giant beast's rhythm.

He had prepared for this most of his life, yet he came to his task a fledgling. At that moment, he felt immeasurably, impossibly small.

Thoughts rushed to his head, and he sensed his heart's rhythmic beating through every nerve in his body. *Thump. Thump. Thump. I could leave now. Ma and Shukra are too busy preparing for the pooja, and Surpanakha is engrossed in deep conversation with Kumbhakarna. I could avoid my inevitable encounter with death or whatever else the aranya, the jungle, has laid out for me.*

Thump. Thump. Thump. It matched the breathing of the forest. *Thump. Thump. Thump.* At that moment, Ravan became painfully aware of his mortality. All those years of preparation had blessed him with extraordinary strength, cunning, even a bit of wisdom, but nothing could prepare him for what lay ahead in the vast aranya.

You could leave now, his mind prodded. *You could leave and avoid death. Live life without rule or obligation. You could escape.* And for a fleeting second, Ravan considered it. He considered giving up, abandoning the privileges that had been bestowed upon him. Then, his secret Teacher's words echoed in his ears: *It is moments of fear that determine who you are. They hold up a mirror to your self and show your essence the truth. Mortality is not a weakness. It is shakti. Strength. It strips you of your armour and forces you to look at yourself as a common Narakan. Prince aside, that is what you are.* Even now, he could see the weight in his secret Teacher's eyes. *But you can choose to be more. Choices are aplenty Ravan. Make the right one.*

The Teacher was right. His words empowered the young Asuran prince; Shiva's strength filled Ravan's body with confidence. *I will return from the forest twice-born. Dvija. Shukra gives too much importance to the Trial. He says it's my only path to mastery.* Ravan's secret Teacher had laughed at the finality of that assessment. *Mastery isn't some armour you put on, nor an unusual talisman you fight for and wear about your neck,* he had said. *Mastery is the journey of many lifetimes, not a reward for mere survival in the Trial.*

The day you accept responsibility for your words, thoughts, actions—that is the day you become an adult. And the day you take the lives of others as your responsibility and guard them as your own? That day you become a twice-born Asuran.

His secret Teacher's words demanded attention, as if the older man were right there, whispering in his ear. *Not Shukra, not the one who teaches us the art of state and war and literature, natural sciences and etiquette and philosophy in the Siddhi Nivas, the Hall of Mastery. Not Shukra, guru of the Asuran royals, to whom my sister, Surpanakha, my brother, Kumbhakarna, and our cousins bow to our daily lessons.*

No. Ravan had another master, a Teacher to whom his mother had secretly taken him, even as a child. *In anticipation of the Trial, my Teacher has been instrumental in ways Shukra could never be.*

"Yuvaraja Ravan. We must proceed." Chief Priest Shukra, guru of all noble Asurans, was a tall and hawk-nosed man. The ornaments of his office—silver and gold and flashing ruby—dangled from silk raiment. He was not overly given to cheer, his rare smile akin to a painful grimace for most.

He was not smiling now. Instead, as he poured honey and milk over the smooth, cylindrical granite lingam of their God, he chanted:

सर्व सुगन्ध सुलेपिथ लिङ्गम |
बुद्धि विवर्धन कारण लिङ्गम ||
सिद्ध सुरासुर वन्दित लिङ्गम |
तत् प्रणामि सदाशिव लिङ्गम ||

(I bow before that Sada Shiva Linga,
Lavishly smeared with variegated perfumes and scents,
That which elevates the power of thought and enkindles the light of discrimination,
And before which the Siddhas and Asurans prostrate.)

"My prince, you must now stand and pronounce the mantras, the words of initiation," he intoned. "Your spirit, your *aatma*, awaits its destiny."

"Er, right, Purohita Shukra," Ravan said, adjusting the silken white dhoti wrapped around his legs and knotted at the waist as he stood up. "I was just pondering a moment."

"Destiny, destiny, destiny. Hmm bah!" muttered Surpanakha, Ravan's younger sister and more insolent sibling. The impudence that Ravan and Kumbhakarna nurtured in the safety of their minds, Surpanakha felt free to say aloud. They had paid for it time and again, brothers and sister. "Can we get the mantras and fancy speeches over with, so he can say goodbye to his family?"

"It's not goodbye," Kumbhakarna hissed. "He's coming back. Don't say it's goodbye."

Surpanakha snorted in irritation, and in a smooth, practised motion, adjusted her voluminous silk sari and moved over to sit behind Ravan, performing her best 'noblewoman's affronted huff.'

It wasn't good acting. Surpanakha did a good affronted huff, but not much of what she did could be called noble-womanly. Instead, Surpanakha was flash and fire and full of the music of veena strings.

"Princess," Chief Priest Shukra admonished, "you are not to approach your brother during the Intonation of the Trial of Seven Days as he utters the sacred mantras. However, familial farewells are permitted later, an integral part of the Trial ceremony."

Surpanakha huffed and stalked back to Queen Kaikesi, several yards away.

And Father choosing not to come from the Nagan battlefront? Ravan wondered silently. *Is that an integral part of the Trial ceremony?*

"Ravan," the priest said as he poured ghee into the fire, "please chant the sacred mantras."

Ravan sighed and nodded, turning once more to face the jungle from his seat at the Shri Mahadev Yaagamandapa Temple, a jewel of his city, Lanka, its walls adorned with frescoes of the life of Shiva the Destroyer.

The forest breathed and reached and waited. As it always did.

"I come here a boy, born and strengthened by the blood and wisdom of my fathers." The words rolled off Ravan's tongue like the lightest laugh, as natural as breathing. But his heart was far away. "I come here to test myself against the aranya and to rise above its challenges. The spirit of my forefathers, Pulastyasura and Shankasura, and that of my father, Vishravasura dwells within me. Shiva, Destroyer of Evil, ever infuses me with courage. I am a noble Asuran, and all I need is within me. I shall not fail. For my forefathers. For my family. For Lanka."

Ravan's words diffused from his lips as lamplight diffuses across an entire room from a bright diya. Their effect seemed to drift out across the temple, the palace gardens, the plains and then, to his surprise, he felt the leaves of the aranya in the distance stir ever so slightly in response.

The jungle waited.

Having uttered the sacred words, he stood silently as Shukra murmured the final mantras of the Shiva pooja and signed the customary marks across his body.

You are small as the leaf is small. As the ant is small. As the viper is small. Each in the way of its nature, the way of its perfection.

Only, Ravan wasn't a leaf. An ant. Or even a viper.

Ravan was a noble Asuran. *Each in the way of its perfection.*

"It does not matter that I am an intruder in the jungle," Ravan murmured, "because mine is a more powerful realm."

"What did you say?" Chief Priest Shukra asked, stony brows furrowing into a scowl.

"I need to say goodbye now," Ravan said, turning back to his family without waiting for the chief priest's word. No need to wait. *I know the ritual by heart. I can leave without offending Mahadeva.*

First, he hugged Kumbhakarna, tall and sombre in his scarred duelling leathers. Ever practical, Ravan's brother hadn't bothered to change into the customary silk dhoti and *angarkha* jacket. Kumbhakarna would be back at practice just as soon as the ceremony ended. It wasn't that he didn't care for Ravan—very much the opposite. It was just that he couldn't reverse what had been set into motion. He'd known the Trial was coming and processed his emotions as best he could. Kumbhakarna would ride out the storm of worry he felt for Ravan by throwing himself into study and practice. That was Kumbhakarna's way. By training hard and long in the martial and magical arts of his nation.

Not so Surpanakha.

"Maybe I can meet up with you after the pooja!" she'd urged the night before, in one of her relentless attempts. "I can slip out of the city palace through the southeast peacock gate before anyone knows I'm gone, and we can face the aranya toge—"

"That's cheating, Surpanakha," Ravan had interrupted with a sigh. "As is giving me secret weapons, extra supplies, or Father's atharva talismans. Cheating will disqualify me."

"Only if you're caught. Only if they know."

"I'll know." With conviction. "Whether I'm caught or not, it doesn't matter. Either way, I won't have completed the Trial. Either way, I won't be twice-born. . . "

* * *

"Brother!" Surpanakha's laugh transported him back to the present. She prodded him playfully, smudging the three horizontal lines of sacred ash on his bare chest. Despite her attempts at levity, the dusky lilac paint across her eyelids was streaked with tears. She brushed them away. "Not drifting off already, are you, brother? That comes later, when the wily monster, Mohini, snares you with a seductive look and drinks all your heart's bleeding love until you die."

"Ever encouraging, sister." He tried to gild his voice with the lightness they customarily shared but could not overcome the gravity of the moment.

I'm not afraid of dying. Not even of failing. No. What I'm deeply afraid of is what they will all think if I should fail. Of the twisted fury on Father's face.

"You come back to us safe and sound, foolish *kushmanda* melon. . . " Surpanakha whispered, jabbing him again. "This is what you get for wanting to be the earliest twice-born among us."

Ravan forced a laugh. His sister's humour suffered when she was worried. "Hey, I'm no fool and hardly twice-born or dvija yet, Surpanakha. Not yet. Give me a week."

And at last, his mother, Kaikesi, always dignified and gentle. Her eyes, brimming with tears, burned into his. *The most beautiful eyes I've ever seen. They give me everything I need in this moment.*

"Mother." He smiled weakly.

"You come back to me," she whispered, enfolding him in her embrace and kissing him upon the brow. "You come back to me strong and dvija, my future maharaja."

"Come, my prince," Chief Priest Shukra intoned. His voice was softer but only slightly.

Ravan went, stooping on the way to pick up his supplies: a light store of salted and dried goat meat jerky (*mamsa*), a buffalo skin water bag called a *masaka*, his hunting *khukri* knives, a light-weight bronze *dhanush* or bow, and several bronze-tipped arrows. The final hymns were then sung by Shukra's brahmin bards, three horizontal lines of sacred ash applied upon his forehead, and a concluding round of prayers made to Lord Shiva.

When the *yagna,* the sacrifice, was complete, Chief Priest Shukra nodded. Ravan turned and bowed, once, to all the people watching. Their faces reduced to pale blurs, their multi-coloured lehengas, saris, and angarkhas melding together into a haze of insignificance.

His family was solemn. Watching.

Then he turned, walked out of the southeast Mayur Raajadhvaara, the peacock gate of the great city his father had built, and let himself be swallowed by the forest.

Thus, did Ravan, firstborn of Vishravasura, sovereign of Asurans on Naraka, begin his twice-born dvija trial.

A few hours passed. The jungle deepened. Rosewood, banyan, *shaala,* and dipterocarp trees became taller, older, more brooding. With the rising canopy, the wind grew distant, gliding with a whisper far above, leaving the underside filled only with the insufferable heat and cacophony of the jungle.

The timbre of the noise changed as well. *In the outer parts, near my beloved kingdom, it is a lighter and softer thing, dampened by Asurankind's weight upon the realm. Here, though, farther in, everywhere are explosions of birdsong, the churr of insects, and the barking and screeching chaos of the howler monkeys.*

As he rounded a bend fringed with a large limestone boulder overgrown with thunbergia vines, he tripped on a tree root and fell flat on his face in the dirt. Angrily picking himself up, he brushed the dust from his eyes, and that's when he saw the high mark on a tree in front of him. A giant bolt of lightning in white painted on the most massive shaala he had ever seen.

The Devan sign to turn back. To go past the sign is forbidden to all Narakans. At that moment, Ravan felt the jungle thrumming through him, an infinity of lives woven together so thick and inextricable that they formed one vast, primeval breathing melody.

To go forward is only peril.

"I will be alright," Ravan asserted as he bounded forth past the shaala, rounding a hilltop and pausing to take his bearings. "There's nothing I can't handle with my dhanush, my khukris, and Asuran magic. I just need to remember what the Teacher and Shukra have taught me." *Listen to the beasts of the ground, the fowl of the air, the insects on the trees, and read their signs. Understand their ways of thinking yet keep yourself above them. Become the wild and yet remain distinct. Play the melodies of the aranya when it suits you and rise above them when it does not.*

The role of the dvija, Shukra whispered in his ear, *To take dominion over Asurapura and nurture it to fullness. To rule it with strength and understanding, ripening all things in their way, and pruning all things as they become unneeded.*

Ravan snorted. *I like Shukra well enough, but the man is only a common high priest. He isn't anything like my secret Teacher.*

"How can we gain dominion over Asurapura," the prince muttered, "if we can't even gain dominion over ourselves?" Out here, alone in the aranya, he could speak freely of his feelings towards the hated Devan conquerors. After their victories in the great battles and The Accords that followed, the Devas had demanded that Naraka bow to their emperor, Indra's rule. For hundreds of years, four of Naraka's five races had continued to do so. Devan officials had become an integral part of every kingdom's hierarchy, interwoven through chains of command of the ruling houses of the Asuras, Rakshasas, Nagas, or Vidyadharas. The Kinnaras were too wild and warlike to be subdued even by the Devas.

The four so-called civilized realms of Naraka were content to build massive defensive forts with Devan help at the edges of their domains to keep the marauding Kinnaras at bay without invading Kinnaran abodes—the vast steppe to the northwest and the already impenetrable desert that lay to the west.

Thankfully, the nobles were largely left to their own devices, free to govern their people and enjoy the luxuries of aristocracy as they wished, so long as they honoured Deva sovereignty and paid the heavy tribute, or *bali.*

Then there were the overlords, the aloof Prajapatis. Though technically responsible for governing the fourteen realms, they mostly seemed content to observe from their high perch as Naraka's conflicts ran their course—again, so long as everything went smoothly.

So long as things go smoothly for the Devas, Ravan thought bitterly. *The Prajapatis don't seem to care much if the realms of Naraka tear each other apart. So long as they feel 'balance' is preserved on the continents of Naraka, Swarga, and Bhooloka. Whatever 'balance' means.*

"*Pitr* really should have come," he told himself, hitching his supplies higher on his back and heading off down the hill. *Father..* . Ravan felt a wave of anger rising in his belly, of familiar scorn towards the king. And then, with a deep breath, he swore and shifted his focus back to the trail.

The game trail ahead was little more than a scratch of dust through a band of *aam* trees, and overgrown vines so thick they looked like they might suffocate him if he tried walking through them. The jungle was hopelessly chaotic, and Ravan knew he had to find clean water before the day was done.

Priority one? Shukra would demand during their monthly training runs in the aranya.

"Water, fresh and running." The prince sighed and slapped away an obnoxious fly, wishing it were a mosquito. Mosquitos meant water was close, though usually stagnant. Theoretically.

"All I've got is bloody theories," he muttered. "Theories and hours of being stalked by Shukra in this jungle and having to evade him. I've never had to escape from a wild *makara water demon* or a hungry lion."

The mango trees, heavy with delicious looking aam were silent, swallowing his words without reply. They waited. His skin tingled every time he thought of this for too long, so he forged ahead and focused on his thoughts.

Priority two? Shukra would continue.

Shelter. Ravan grunted, pushing through the dense foliage, until suddenly, he found himself at a ridge overlooking a rather steep valley, beyond which lay another small hill. *If there isn't water in this valley, there will certainly be some at the next.*

He hoped to find a pool, follow the stream that fed it up to a precise point, and then look for an elevated outcropping nearby upon which to form a shelter.

One that affords both safety and a view. If I had to choose, I'd take the vantage point. He didn't care if his enemies came; he only wanted to see them coming. It was the place of Nagas to hide—the hybrid snake-Narakan species. And of *mooshika,* fearful mice.

The role of the twice-born dvija, he chanted in his mind. *To take dominion over Asurapura and nurture it to fullness.*

Ravan was sure he was on his way to being twice-born as he carefully navigated down the ridge. *Still, even twice-born princes have fathers, and Pitr should have come.*

It was as if Lord Vishravasura had centuries' worth of Narakan anger boiling inside him. Because he couldn't direct it at its source—the Devas—he let it flail wildly across his realm, sparking conflict where peace might reign, launching wars against the Nagas and Rakshasas. *Instead of transmuting it, perhaps even with Asuran magic, into love. Love for his family. Love for me, his eldest son.*

Someday, perhaps, Father will dissolve his anger and remember the daily trials and tribulations of his subjects, his family, his kin—and that of his firstborn.

The valley he entered didn't have a water source in the end, but a red-faced *malkoha* cuckoo with a long, graduated green tail greeted Ravan with repeated high-pitched shrieks at the Asuran prince's intrusion. The valley beyond that was even steeper, with Ravan sweating profusely as he pushed onward. He finally arrived at a pool, but it was small and dank and filled from everywhere at once. From tiny chinks in the rocks, dripping symphonies from long-legged crickets, and frogs sitting on moss-covered stones. A streamlet that arrived from up-valley trickled into the pool.

Sighing and adjusting his quiver, Ravan forged upstream. Barking deer and blue magpies announced his presence to the rest of the aranya. His trek upstream didn't seem to promise much better, but it was the best chance he had.

In the end, he traversed narrow jungle passages up two more ridges and three more valleys before he found fresh water. The sun had not yet set; he considered it a day well utilized. The spring gurgled, sparkling, bubbling up from the hillside on a pad of verdant moss, frogs and skinks scrambling away as he arrived.

The broad, bald face of a massive granite boulder thrust up from the base of a grove of shaala trees on the edge of the flowing water. Relieved, Ravan clambered around and up, shrugging off his dhanush, quiver, masaka, and khukris with a sigh.

I pushed myself hard today. Too hard, perhaps. Shukra would have disapproved, and Mother would certainly have thrown a fit.

The Teacher, however, would have grinned and nodded slowly, clapping that characteristic clap. It was a gesture that made him uncertain about whether he was being mocked or praised. *Nevertheless, my lessons with the Teacher since I was a child prepared me for this very day.*

Ravan was glad he'd found water. *The goat mamsa jerky will keep hunger at bay for at least another day.*

He'd been trained for this, surviving for days and nights in the jungle on roots, berries, and wild bananas. He'd even gone a spell without water—a full forty hours until the Teacher had threatened to hang him by his ears if he didn't stop.

Even the Teacher shows compassion on occasion, he thought with a wry grin. Lately, the wise old man didn't seem to push Ravan as hard as the prince pushed himself.

I will conquer the Trial and return home triumphant. Twice-born, making my father and ancestors proud. Then, Father will perhaps regret the fact that he doesn't even know the man I've become.

As the sun dipped to touch the horizon, spilling out its molten brilliance and burning up the western sky, Ravan set his camp in order. First, he cut himself a supple thunbergia vine and hung his pack and masaka on a branch of the shaala nearest the boulder, where none but those strong enough to break through treated leather might hope to reach. Then he shouldered his bow and descended to the spring, drinking a couple of mouthfuls before rescaling the rock and settling down in a meditative *kamala,* or lotus position, his back to the jungle, facing out over the foliage from his clifflike perch.

Picking up his *rudraksha* beads, he closed his eyes, breathed deep *ujjayi* yoga breaths, and let his being flow through his body and out into the surroundings. Using the name of Neelakanta, the One who had swallowed the deadly poison Hala-Hala to save the Universe, Ravan chanted. . .

> मृत्युञ्जयाय रुद्राय नीलकन्ताय शंभवे |
> अमृतेषाय सर्वाय महादेवाय ते नमः ||
>
> (Oh Lord Rudra-Shiva, you are the one who has conquered death and are responsible for the destruction of the Universe to let life again prevail on earth.
> Oh Lord, you are Neelakanta, as you have a blue throat. We pay obeisance to you, Lord, with our hands folded in namaskar.)

High Priest Shukra would probably call chanting at a time and place like this foolish. But Shukra knows not the least of my abilities, nothing of the white and dark arts I have learned and mastered under the Teacher's tutelage. Chanting a joining mantra through his mind, Ravan wove himself through the forest. *I feel every fibre of energy around me. The energy that flows through the roots of trees all around me. The energy of the wind on the leaves, that of animals large and small.* He felt it all, and yet he kept himself distinct. Always, when they spoke of meditation, the great seers and rishis spoke of being One—of connecting to the Divine that was in all creation.

But the Teacher and I keep ourselves distinct. Nature is Divine, and yes, I am part of creation. But I am not merely the essence of the jungle—I am much more. I am the spear tip, the pinnacle of consciousness, the highest kalasa, or finial, of the great temple of Asurankind.

I am the Divinity and the Being and the Purpose, and the Teacher has taught me that I am right to keep myself distinct.

Ravan climbed back to the boulder. Just as he fully began to settle in, he grew bored. Perhaps two hours had passed, no more. The Teacher would not have been pleased with his impatience.

But there was just so much life around him. He couldn't weave himself through the forest and then ignore it. He had to *feel* it.

Darkness fell during his spiritual vigil. The utter cacophony of jungle life that was the night made the chaos of the day seem dull. Insects were everywhere, churring and clicking, agamids and beetles, all adding their sounds to the symphony. Bullfrogs thundered in the water below, and the shuffling of a somewhat larger creature disturbed the brush off to one side. Probably a deer, for it moved away quickly.

The canopy stretched out below him, the mantle of the dark sky bathed by stars.

Hmm, he thought, curling up with his bow and arrows close to hand. *Tomorrow I'll work on a shelter first thing, but tonight, the cloudless sky promises not to send its usual downpour.*

He kept a tendril of thought half alert, weaving another mantra in a breathing-dream state. If anything came to bother him, he'd be able to react swiftly.

Still, rather less action than I'd expected. Isn't this place supposed to hide pit vipers, lions, and other perilous dangers? At the palace, he had the company of Surpanakha's constant wit, his mother's nagging, and Shukra's strict rules.

Hmm. . . perhaps the beings of the aranya sense my powers and stay away.

Chapter 2

The Way the Lotus Burns

Surpanakha was livid. *No. Livid isn't the right word. Irritated, though that, too, is a touch off.*

"Miffed, perhaps," she said, nodding at its sound. "I'm miffed. By Kaala, Harsha. If he does it anymore, I'll get irritated, and then it's far beyond livid. I'll explode. I'll *kill* him."

"That would be a thing to see." Harsha grinned. "The daughter of the Maharaja going at it with High Priest Shukra, head of all Shiva temples on Naraka."

"You just *watch* me," she growled. "He tries anything like that with me, and you'll see it soon enough." Shukra had said her brother, Kumbhakarna, was 'sulking' about Ravan facing the Trial before *he* could. Sulking, when the younger prince ought to have thanked the ancient *shaastras,* or laws, for their clear stipulation that the eldest son of the king attempted the Trial first.

Sulking, by which Shukra meant Kumbhakarna had been devoting more time to practising sword fighting with his *khanda,* his double-edged straight sword, and less to performing fire sacrifices. *A noble decision,* she thought.

"The shaastras say only boys get to perform fire sacrifices and learn battle spells," she complained. "As far as I can see, chattering into the sacrificial fire and paying fat, bald men who sit around and chant all day is hardly helpful. Much better to practise sparring with Uncle Akampana. That way, if Ravan does manage to survive the Trial of Seven Days but can't find his way back, we'll be prepared to go in and save him when he needs it."

"Fat, bald men, who sit around and chant all day?" Harsha looked horrified. "Those aren't the words you *used*, right?"

Surpanakha sniffed and glanced away. "Well," she muttered, "I may have thrown in an adjective or two."

"But you called Shukra's priests *fat*?"

"सत्यमेव जयते नानृतं | Truth ultimately triumphs, not falsehood, the Vedas say."

"And bald!"

"सत्येन विधृतं सर्वं सर्वं सत्ये परतिष्ठितम | Everything is upheld by truth, and everything rests upon truth, so say or do it even if it's hard, the Vedas say."

"And you said the ancient laws wouldn't help?" Harsha clutched his head in both hands and looked away, muttering in distress.

"Look!" Surpanakha snapped. "Shukra was getting on my nerves. He's always saying our ancestors *watch*. They *judge*. And he accused me of trying to supply Ravan with special weapons and talismans."

"You were," Harsha pointed out.

"Yes, but Ravan would never *take* them! He's far too noble. Shukra should know that by now."

"Ah. So you're offended on Ravan's account, not yours."

"Exactly."

"Ever the selfless *saadhvi*." Harsha enfolded her in his bronzed arms, thrumming with the warmth and vigour of the Sun Elemental. He'd packed away the warm *chuba*, the traditional Vidyadharan robe and felt trousers necessary for his ride from the Peaks and put on a cotton robe and pants. Surpanakha liked the way his bare arms flexed when they held her. She savoured the subtle ways the muscles of his forearms danced across her stomach. She adored his musk.

"I don't know why mother makes me wear a sari every day," she pouted. "All these drapes and paints and heavy gold jewellery. It's like I'm a *mani-pradipa*, a chandelier, not a person. How am I supposed to climb down?" She jerked a thumb, indicating their perch high on a giant shaala at the edge of the aranya, where Harsha had flown them on his *pisacha*, Uluka. His dragon allowed him to travel high in the clouds as he explored the far reaches of Naraka. The Vidyadharan prince lived as one with the high Peaks of the northeast, vast forests of deodar and pine trees. A simpler life, trying to rediscover the fundamental ways of Narakankind. As did the *sapta kula*, the seven clans of his people.

As Harsha would put it, "Rediscovering a life of Oneness with Goddess Shakti." So many ancient ways, Songs, and bonds with the One had been lost. All he had was his bond with Uluka.

Surpanakha loved everything about him. The way he doted on his pisacha. His fluency with Samskritam, the Asuran language, for another. *Were all Vidyadharan tribes multi-lingual?* Surpanakha wondered.

Harsha gave himself entirely to the creed of his people, holding nothing back. The Vidyadharas had found early in the development of their civilization that all of nature is interconnected. They believed from their earliest days that interconnection—whether material, social, or political—was the key to their survival as a race.

His deep love of his people and their ways makes him passionate and fierce but also gentle, innocent, and kind, Surpanakha thought. Her own brothers, Ravan and Kumbhakarna, were mostly fire and passion. They took after Father. *Pitr. . .*

"Surpanakha, look at me," his breath was warm upon her bejewelled neck.

She glanced up at him.

"I see you," he said. "I see your worry. I see how deeply you care for Ravan. But don't let your worry eat you up. Don't fear for your *jyeshta's* life. Far weaker men than your elder brother have made it a week in the jungle. Ravan will survive."

"I'm not worried!" She protested. "I'm—"

"Right now, you're wielding a tongue as sharp and as childish as your cousin Dushana," he chuckled. "Everyone knows you have a sharp wit. But when you're childish like this, I know something's amiss. You're trying to mask your worry. But look at me. No, really, look at me. Ravan will be safe. Say it."

She sighed and stuck out her tongue but quickly turned away before he could see her tearing up. *The truth is, he doesn't know how terrified I am for Ravan's safety. I feel helpless.* "If my father knew you'd whisked me away from the roof of my mother's abode, from the maharani's palace to bring me here," she said, "he'd surely have me confined to my rooms."

"If your pitr knew I came to visit you at all," Harsha said drily, "I think we'd have bigger worries. So, when are you going to tell your father we are. . . " he trailed off, indicating the surrounding foliage with a shrug.

"That we're sitting high up on a tree on the edge of the aranya?" she asked, a playful twinkle in her eyes. *What is it about men that makes them so hesitant to call this what it is?*

"Well, we are. . . we are *seeing* each other."

"Hah! *Seeing?" Oh, Shiva. I really ought to punch him for that.* Straight out of the tree.

"Well, what do you call what we're doing?" the Vidyadharan prince demanded.

"I. . . well. . . " Words seemed to escape her for the moment. "I asked *you*," she sniffed. "And besides, I'm worried about Ravan, remember?"

"So, you *are* worried."

* * *

Day Two

As was his habit, Ravan's mind stirred before Surya, the Sun Elemental, arose. For about an hour, he meditated on the jungle, remaining still in his *shavaasan,* or sleeping yoga pose. He meditated on the wind rustling through the light-leafed branches. On how it wrought a softer melody through the broad, heavy leaves of the shaala and torchwood trees. On how it whispered over the granite boulder and gently kissed his skin.

It tells me secrets, the wind. Stories of the jungle's heart, of the animals it sees and the scents they give off—fear and hunger and rut—and of the weather that it bears. He cast a spell to ward off the ever-eager mosquitoes and other insects of the jungle. Ravan didn't quite know how the wind had carried the essence of the jungle to him. His secret Teacher had told him the spirit would reveal itself to anyone who meditated. Shukra said that even a commoner could do this if he chanted the mantras and sacrificed at the right temples, worshipping the Destroyer.

The Teacher sneered at that and called it a fraud of religion. *The universe's melody runs through every living thing. But in some,* he said, *it is awake. Ravan, you have the potential to become powerfully, shockingly—*

"Awake." Ravan snapped his eyes open to greet the sunlight. *It's going to be a hot spring day. I've made it through one day. Six more to go.*

Quickly, he did his morning routine, darting through the jungle to limber up. Then, hatha yoga poses and pranayama.

By the time the Sun Elemental had detached himself fully from the horizon, Ravan was warm and well alert, a light film of sweat covering his body. He trotted over to the stream, washed himself, and did his *sandhya vandana* prayers. He then uttered a mantra:

> शं नो ढेवी रभिष्टय आपो भवन्तु पीतये ।
>
> (May these wholesome waters be a source of pleasure to us for healthy drinking.)

Satisfied the water in the spring below was now pure, he untied his supplies and quenched his thirst before refilling his masaka from the clear stream.

The first order of business, to find more food. I can easily survive a few days without eating—thanks to my Teacher's training—but I should be able to eat like a Maharaja in this jungle of plenty. Especially since creatures in the deep aranya rarely see us. Well, maybe not rarely.

Villagers probably came through to pick fruit, maybe wilder Nagas, straying far from their nests to hunt, or else exiled by their kin and banished to the jungle. They were a wild bunch that frequently squabbled amongst themselves. It wasn't uncommon to hear of a wilder Naga heading off to live in the forest alone in serpentform.

But they can hardly be called evolved beings, whether in serpentform or narakanform. Their thinking, their scent, and even their magic is just a touch. . . primeval.

Ravan's lips twisted sourly. He had experienced enough of Nagas, especially female Nagas, after studying alongside his fellow student, Vaasuki, under the Teacher's careful eye. But that was the way of the Teacher. Mysterious and warped, refusing to consider commonly accepted rules of culture and sophistication. Or even those of nature.

But anyway, prey should be available aplenty and quite easily caught, even without magic. Most of these animals have probably never smelled an Asura.

That was the exact moment, of course, when he heard the shouts. Shouts in a strange language.

Ravan stiffened, scrambling back against the boulder, peering over it carefully. Nothing.

I need to get back to my supplies without being seen. . .

He heard more shouts, accompanied by a distinct cracking noise. *A breaking branch?* Another crack, accompanied by raucous laughter. *Whoever it is, they're a large group.*

Hurriedly, Ravan scrambled over the open ground toward his weapons. Dhanush in hand and quiver at the ready, he belted on his bronze khukris and pack, and wriggled back to the boulder.

The possibility that the band was friendly never entered his mind. *This is the aranya, where strangers are either predators or prey. I'm on my own.*

Whoever they are, best they pass by, not knowing I'm here. He was reasonably certain that the group was downhill from him, but sounds were tricky as they bounced off the valley and its trees. *I'd better—*

There. He saw them just across the slope, a series of pale heads bobbing above the brush as they followed a game trail over a series of calcified limestone boulders. They bore large leather packs on their backs.

Interesting. Packs. They aren't Narakans—none of the races of Naraka ever stray this far from their interior lands, and certainly not with equipage as sophisticated as this.

Wilder Nagas, perhaps? But doing what? Whatever it is, those packs are likely stuffed with food.

And they were vulnerable to his bow and his magic.

Stomach growling softly at the thought, Ravan crouched lower and followed their movements. *I wouldn't need to hunt, not if an entire troop's rations fell into my hands. . .*

I don't want to kill them, of course. Ravan had killed the odd criminal before—one sentenced to death—as part of his training. Public executions weren't uncommon under Asuran law.

My khukris have been tested in combat against the royal radgachars, the nearly invincible gladiators of Lanka. With his bow and arrow. With spear and khanda, under the able tutelage of his uncle, Arch BladeRanger Akampana. He had beaten many and rarely been defeated in the Ring of Trying.

Is this the real Trial? The thought made his blood run hotter. His forearms tingled with anticipation. *Ravan, the peril of the jungle.*

Then he saw the glint of iron. Tall warriors with flaxen hair, carrying halberds, iron axe blades topped with spikes mounted on long shafts. With nasty-looking hooks on the obverse side to grapple with horsemen. Then, as one stepped high on a rock, the prince also saw the glint at the warrior's waist—an iron quillon dagger.

A chill ran down Ravan's spine, and he hissed in alarm, dropping below the rock line and scrambling back to the spring.

Devas. The only beings on Naraka permitted to carry iron.

Devas. The conquerors, not only of his people but also of sizable kingdoms belonging to four of five races on Naraka.

What are you doing, idiot? he asked himself, his stomach churning. *One moment you were going to stay away and let them pass. Smart. But the next, you're thinking of ambushing them and stealing their food?*

Surpanakha is right. I can be a fool, a moorkha sometimes.

Keep your head, Ravan! He strapped on his quiver and brushed his fingers along the feathers of goose-fletched arrows. The feeling was comforting, familiar. He'd done it a thousand times. His aim was unerring. He would fell chital, or sambhar, or boar almost every time. But these were *adult* Devan warriors.

"So, think!" He cursed, inching back up the rock and watching as the last of the Devas faded into an enormous grove of teak trees across the way.

The young man trembled. *I've trained for the hunt. To track animals. To battle Rakshasas and Nagas. But I haven't trained for adult Devan warriors—expert halberdiers, longbowmen, masters of the magic of Lord Brahma. And of Swargan battle tactics. They are the dominants over the kingdoms of Naraka. If they catch me out here in the forbidden part of the aranya. . . The Devas have warded this area with magic, so even Vidyadharan pisachas can't fly over it.*

After a time, his heartbeat slowed and his blood ceased to burn hot. The Devas were gone, and nothing had happened.

Images of torture, of endless punishment for disobedience to Chakravarthi Indra, faded from his mind.

He was all alone in the valley.

Cursing himself for being a weak-kneed fool, Ravan set off to look for suitable game in a direction away from where the Devas had disappeared. Within minutes, he found fresh tracks and within the hour, he had tracked down and shot a sambhar. It was a young and medium-sized buck.

He then built a fire of heavy, dense ironwood. He proceeded to dig a circular fire pit around the fire, knowing the ironwood would burn slowly and hardly smoke. The smoke that did emerge, he used magic to waft towards his hanging meat. *I'll have to keep guard against predators or Devas.* The meat smelled like the seven heavens of the Prajapatis as he turned it over the fire, his stomach grumbling in ravenous anticipation.

As the mamsa cooked, he hummed a tune: "The Way the Lotus Burns." *Mother's favourite lullaby. A simple piece by sound, it calms me as always. I used to think the lyrics were simple, but I now know they are not.* They spoke of emotions, dark and sorrowful.

His brow furrowed as he thought of his father. *Father knows no lullabies. The only songs Pitr knows are ballads of war.* Ravan longed for his father's love, his attention. But there would be none thrown his way. At that moment, there was much of the realm that seemed sorrowful, dark, and lonely. He shook his head and turned his attention back to his meal.

He wished he had some honey to soak the meat in, to cook it into sweet mamsa jerky. *Perhaps I should have looked for beehives,* he mused. *Or tried to use mango nectar from the aam trees as a marinade.*

The heart and liver of the young buck the prince ate in full, stuffing himself until his stomach strained outward, full as a sugarcane field before harvest on the southern Rakshasan islands. *Some might call it a foolish thing to stuff oneself with potential predators about. But I have magic and can handle even lions. Better to restore my physical strength as fast as possible with a meal rich in protein.*

He sat back and relaxed, waiting for his engorged stomach to settle before completing his shelter. Night came just as he finished the roof of his shelter with feather-palm leaves he found on the aranya floor. Casting a mantra of protection on his shelter, the prince settled down to a deep and troubled sleep, dreaming of Devan warriors burning down his father's Chandra Rajakula Palace in the heart of Lanka.

Day Three

At dawn, Ravan rose, still perturbed by the previous night's events. The aranya had thoroughly entered his mind. *There is a darkness to my thoughts that don't belong, not out here, not under the great canopy of the aranya, while kissed by spring's breeze.*

Tonight, he vowed, *I'll sleep better. The Teacher has trained me to do my karma, my duty, without fear.* He finished is morning ablutions, prayers, and routine quickly and quietly.

The hours passed uneventfully as he laboured to build a better shelter. First, he cleared the ground between two massive shaala trees growing uphill of his boulder. Then he found a stand of teak saplings nearby, young and straight. Using them, he created the frame for his lean-to. Then he felled two dozen teak saplings, leaning them one by one against his crossbeam until he'd erected a simple structure. He jammed them together as tightly as possible, then secured them with thunbergia vines at the tips on each side and sank their bases several inches into the loose jungle soil.

Once he had finished with the bare frame, he created a hasty plaster with a mixture of clay-like soil and coarse grasses—no straw was to be found—then sealed the lean-to and left it time to dry.

Finally, he used the dark, fibrous bark and leaves of the feather palm, broad and heavy as sheets of metal. Ravan completely covered his shelter with the leaves, layering and tying them together. Last came a series of traps surrounding his dwelling that ought to snare any predator that sought to ambush him.

He passed the remainder of the day packing the dried meat of the sambhar, then climbed the surrounding trees and explored their fruit. The howler monkeys were possessive of 'their' trees. They had teeth that were long, sharp, and dirty, perfect for infecting weak-bodied Asuran prey.

Still, they had not the will to chase him once he shot their leader with an arrow. The trees around his boulder were his, and he marked his conquest with the blood of their fallen leader. *That'll keep them at bay.*

When night came again, he slept, and this time, his sleep was undisturbed. When he awoke the next morning, the spectre of Devan warriors seemed a distant dream.

Then the second party arrived, and this time, he did not hear them until they were nearly on top of him.

Chapter 3

Chains

Day Four

Ravan snapped into full wakefulness at the sound of voices and scrabbled desperately for his bow. He nocked an arrow reflexively.

The prince crouched at the mouth of his lean-to, clutching his dhanush as he fought to calm his quivering muscles. As his heart beat faster, he chanted:

> वितर्क बधने प्रतिपक्श भवनम् ।
>
> (Upon being harassed by negative thoughts, cultivate counteracting thoughts.)

You cannot fight when tense, the teacher had counselled him. *You can battle when you are hurt or tired. Not if you are tense.*

The muscles slow, he heard the Teacher whisper in his mind, *pain expands, the blood flows too fast. It weakens you in every way. You lose an entire layer of intuition and muscle memory.*

But how do you hit hard with relaxed muscles? Ravan had asked.

You strike with savagery, the right muscles taut at the right moment, the old man responded gently. *But until the moment of impact, the body is fluid and loose. When you parry, you block with the strength needed; when you—*

"Focus, moorkha, you idiot!" Ravan scolded himself, shaking his head and returning to the moment. His legs were bent beneath him, the bow held out in front. His left forearm rested lightly on his knee; the bronze-tipped arrow pointed out of the lean-to, aimed at whoever was beyond.

Loose. Ready. Waiting.

The voices continued, accompanied by the metallic clinking of light chain-mail armour and. . .

And another sound. . . Ravan crept from his shelter and edged towards the boulder. The rattle that accompanied the clinking of armour was metallic, and fluid, clanging, rippling as the voices passed by. . .

Chains, he realized belatedly, peering up over the edge of the boulder.

The Devas had come back, six of them. This time, he saw clearly who was with them.

Slaves. They were shackled ankle-to-ankle and wrist-to-wrist in iron, marching in a double file. Ravan felt a rush of horror. These weren't the polished Devan diplomats who presented themselves every year at his father's court. *These are slavers.*

The Devas descended to his spring and drank their fill while replenishing their waterskins.

They were a mere fifty metres below him, well within the range of a stone toss. He ducked and huddled against the boulder, listening to them drink in petrified silence, blood thundering in his ears. His instincts screamed at him to run, to shoot, to hide, to do a hundred different things at once. In the end, he simply huddled there and caught his fingers as they trembled on the fibres of his bowstring.

The Devas took an eternity to finish their water break. Shouting and pushing the slaves back into line, the slavers hacked their way through the foliage back up the hill opposite the boulder. As Ravan peered over the boulder, he saw the narrow path they were on. The chained wretches often stumbled, tripping over protruding roots or tangled vines. The fair-haired Devas cursed and struck the lean bodies of their charges, urging them to go faster and prodding them with iron-tipped halberds.

The very last slave in the group was alone, chained to the others by a running line, trailing several paces behind. He was tall and dreadfully frail, ribs jutting sharply from his sides, his face so sunken he had no cheeks to speak of. The wretch's height only accentuated his frailty.

How can anyone become this emaciated? Ravan stared in mounting horror as the poor thing stumbled, tripping over something on the path and pitching forward with a cry. He vanished for a moment from Ravan's view, obscured by vegetation, then reappeared further up the trail thrashing, legs flailing desperately, dragged along the trail by his wrists.

Let him get up! Ravan flinched as the wretch's forearms and face were battered by a rocky section of the trail, then breathed a sigh of relief as the slave scrambled to his feet and trotted forward with the others.

One of the Devas shouted a curse, lashing out with a leather whip. The tail flicked expertly across the old man's back, tearing through his ragged shirt and slicing a perfect line of red across his back.

Ravan winced. *I don't want to see this. I've seen the blood of men in the fighting arena, during sacrificial rites, and when a criminal was whipped at the palace. But this is different. This is brutal, ruthless savagery.*

The old man was helpless. The prince watched as the wretch stumbled again, crying out in a language Ravan could barely identify. *Rakshasan!* One of the slaves turned to catch the wretch as he fell, hoisting him up by his armpits, chest heaving with exertion as he struggled to help the tall, old Rakshasa up.

As they laboured up a hill, Ravan noticed a simple tattoo through the layer of dirt and blood that coated the stronger slave's shirtless torso. The distinct outline of a trident, three prongs curving to meet a staff, which followed the man's spine down to the small of his back. *He's an Asura! Shiva help them.* Ravan shuddered.

Half-dragged, half-stumbling, the old Rakshasa continued on, his shirt staining as he bled. And then, the party disappeared into the trees.

That old man is helpless, I'm not. I have my dhanush and khukris. I had the element of surprise just a few moments ago. And the Asuran with the tattoo. . .

Why had he hesitated? Why had he done nothing? Ravan found himself shaking with frustration and shame, eyes on the vague rift in the trees into which the slavers had vanished. The Devas' chatter faded and then the clanking of chains, and Ravan was left alone with his anger.

Do something, a voice whispered in his mind. *Do something. Follow the Devas. Kill them! Free the slaves.*

"I must survive," Ravan whispered, glancing back at his lean-to. He'd made sure it was well-camouflaged from every angle, but abruptly, he felt exposed.

But no, I am in the aranya to face monsters. To face Kaala, the God of Death, who stalks you on limbs of darkness, or who slithers in deadly silence, who flies on wings as quick as thought.

"What are a couple of Devan slavers compared to a makara, a river demon, or a *bhramari,* a monster bee?" Ravan forced a chuckle, now perched on his boulder, continuing his anxious scan of the brush. "The inner aranya ought to be as alien to the Devas as it is to me. More so, in fact."

Whenever he and father went to pay the yearly bali to High Lord Vayu at the western Devan stronghold, all the guards did, with their iron chain-mail armour and heavy weapons, was whimper and whine about the heat, the dust, the infernal insects. *It is a wonder these people survived on Naraka, much less conquered it.*

"So then, why am I still standing here?" he asked, fingers curling around his horn-and-bamboo composite bow. *I'm such a coward! I ought to track the Devas until they reach the perfect ambush point, then put arrows through their thick necks.*

Arrows. . . then wait until he was sure they were defeated and dying. Walk down and let them see him, meet his eyes before they died. So they would know who it was that brought justice to Naraka. . .

"You're a fool," he said, curling his lip in disgust and turning away. "This is exactly the sort of talk Pitr warned you against all your life. One peek at Devan slavers, and you think you're some sort of hero?"

Regret and shame washed over him like a giant icy wave off the northern Rakshasan seacoast. *I am one naive Asura. All my life, I've lived a life of luxury in a palace. I was blind to think that the commoners of Naraka were treated as well as Asuran nobles by the Devas. . .*

The Devas need us, he remembered his father saying. *They need us to rule the commoners. Without us, there is no link. No bridge. Without Naraka's nobles, its people are only so many mindless peasants, barking for their freedom. Without us nobles, they would rebel. And then, they would die at the hands of the Devas.*

"They need us nobles," Ravan echoed, "our subjects and the Devas need us. They need us to keep order." His father's words. *An excuse? Vishravasura's strategy to maintain power and keep the family line intact?*

Relative power, of course. *The Devas are a much greater power and have been for centuries. But we retain a small measure of it,* his father had assured him.

So what am I thinking—that I'll dash out and slay a band of Devan warriors by myself? There would be retribution. For every Devan murdered—whether by commoner, by noble, or even by the Underground—the lives of seven Narakans from every civilized race would be forfeited. Seven Asuras. Seven Vidyadharas. Seven Rakshasas. Seven Nagas.

In his mind's eye, he saw the wizened slave dragged face first through the dirt, kicked when he could not rise. He saw the whip slicing through the air, heard it snap, saw that slender line of red appear upon the man's frail back.

Ravan's knuckles clenched as he remembered, and he found a fire swelling in his gut. A familiar heat rose in his belly, driving fear away.

The Devas came to take workers and promised to treat them well. They took the labourers away on horseback and cushioned wagons as proud men and women, as living tribute.

Mining is hard work, but we promise to treat them well. Indra's diplomats never spoke of chains, of whips, and of dragging labourers through the jungle.

But no one ever sees the mines, thought Ravan.

Ravan returned to his shelter, his anger glowing hot inside him. He strapped on his khukris and slung his pack and quiver over his back. The arrow he kept nocked to his bowstring. The Asuran prince stepped lightly through the bush as he descended to the spring.

We promise to treat them well.

The Devas had left footprints everywhere, shredding the soft green moss, leaving muddied chaos behind. A line of hacked and battered brush led from the spring back to the same sparse trail the Devas had taken the day before.

Grimly, he forged ahead, following the trail. There was a practical reason for his pursuit. *If I can't fight them, at least I might see where they're going. If forging through the forbidden aranya with Narakans in chains is a regular Devan practice, I need to find out why.*

A few days in the depths of the aranya, and already, my perspective has been upended. Everything I've learned is being tested, but not in the ways I'd expected. I am trained to use my might and magic to survive in the jungle, perhaps face some of my inner demons, but this is different.

They promise to treat our workers well, but they won't let us see the mines. And always, Pitr bows, is silent, and manages to keep his clan from danger.

The best way to defeat a Devan warrior here is to become the jungle, not just to find shelter, to fortify, and then survive predators. But he was no longer engaged in just a struggle to survive the dangers of the primeval forest. Ravan now faced the menace of battle-hardened and bloodthirsty Devan warriors.

He tracked them for what he reckoned was over ten miles. The trail broadened, became hard-packed, as happens with consistent passage, and the otherwise thick vegetation appeared pruned back until it began to form a sort of sideways-growing wall, a tunnel from which the jungle chose to stay away.

The Devas have been coming here for years, perhaps decades. This is indeed an established route.

Could this lead to a mine? Ravan stooped to inspect a hoofprint on the path. *This is odd. The fore-hoof prints appear to have sunk broader and deeper than those of the rear-hoof prints.* In places that would typically be difficult for horses to manoeuvre, there were marks high up on the surrounding branches—rubbed bark, snapped twigs, and springier branches. *Looks like they've been used as handholds higher up than the average ten-foot-tall Rakshasa would be able to reach.*

Asuras and Rakshasas weren't the only races in the Devan slave trains; they were using Kinnaras. *The Free Folk.* Horse-Narakan hybrids who roamed the massive steppes to the northwest. And the Great Narakan Desert in the west.

A mine? A thrill rushed through him but laced with something hotter. A flare of determination combined with a spark of anger.

The Devan mines were something of a myth among Narakans. That the Devas operated them was well known—minerals and metals were the primary reason for the Devan conquest of Naraka. *Despite Surpanakha's insistence that Swargans were nothing more than war-addicted monsters,* Ravan thought wryly.

They'd come to Naraka because they wanted iron, gold, tin, copper, turquoise, as well as cotton and silk—because they were purer and more plentiful than on Swarga. But for centuries, the mines existed in shadow, in horror stories and savage oaths by Devan *akaradhyakshas,* or mine superintendents, to torture and execute any who dared to interfere with their operations. The locations of the fringe mines were well known: Maniraj-Khani, Kaanchana Giri, and Ratnapur, which was on an island off the western coast of Naraka. But those were fortified mini cities, well-defended behind walls built over decades by the invaders. With Narakan help.

The Devas, even with their superior iron weapons and tactics, fear attack by a restless peasant populace or by the wild Kinnaran tribes. And rightly so—the Underground tried to take Ratnapur castle six times, and once, a band of Rakshasan pirates from the north even succeeded, sailing their kurma turtle-boats in from the icy northern seas and storming the island citadel on a dark, new moon night.

The Devas, led by High Lord Agni, had reconquered the castle and the turquoise mine it protected, slaughtered the pirates, and then proceeded to pour molten lead into the eyes of twenty-eight Narakans for every Deva killed at Ratnapur. Seven from each race for every dead Devan warrior, all from noble houses. *For every Deva killed, seven Asuras, seven Nagas, seven Kinnaras, and seven Vidyadharas were executed.*

There hadn't been another uprising after that horror, not for half a century.

Ravan studied the hoofprints with interest, passion aflame in his heart. *All these centuries of Devan rule, and we've never seen the insides of these mines. Devan diplomats come and go, but the tributes only ever disappear. Not one comes back.*

They had only stories. Nightmares of Devan revenge when the Underground sowed mischief.

What if I saw the inside of a mine? What if I could. . .

Could what?

You're a fool, Ravan. His upper lip curled, and he spat, shaking his head, continuing down the trail. *A kushmanda, as Surpanakha says. You're going to follow the trace, find out where they're headed, and then, you're going to retrace your steps and head back to Lanka. Survive, finish the Trial of Seven Days, tell them what you found, and live to fight another day.*

There was logic in that plan. He forged on, knowing deep down why he followed the hated conquerors. *I will be the first to actually see a Devan mine, and that will be my conquest of the Trial of Seven Days.*

Father can't possibly deny my courage then. Not if I am the first—the only Asuran noble—to actually see a Devan mine and live to tell the tale.

As night fell, he heard thunder and lightning above the canopy. The rain fell in great sheets, cutting through the trees like a bronze sickle through grass. Ravan found a secluded thicket on the far side of a hill that bordered the path. He hung his pack, then fashioned himself a hasty barrier with his khukris, weaving sharpened shaala saplings into a sort of thicket-wall. It wouldn't keep out a determined leopard, but it would give him a warning and the time he needed to defend against an invading predator. Ravan cast the usual spell to ward off the ever-present mosquitoes and turned in for the night.

Chapter 4

Akraamaka

Day Five

Like a river that broadens as it reaches the ocean, the trail grew larger by degrees. Slender tributaries joined every half hour or so—strangled scars through the jungle that curled in from the chaos to abruptly enter Ravan's path. All brought signs of further passage.

Then he hit the road. It was as broad as his father's *yuddha yaana,* or war wagon, and flat as the Sabha Nivas floor in Lanka, with tree branches trimmed well back on either side. The Devas had worked assiduously to maintain it.

"Shiva's blood!" Ravan groaned. *If turning back was ever an option, it's long past now. The Devas might have conquered us, but this is still Naraka.* For centuries, the people had told horror stories about the deadly creatures that menaced the aranya, and now, he'd found a Devan road, of all things, arcing through its very centre.

Devas frequenting the inner aranya? Could it be that the jungle is actually far safer than we'd assumed? Could it be that the Devas have nurtured a fear of this place, a foreboding shared by all Narakans?

Why have we bowed so long in silence?

I wonder if Father knows, he mused, hitching his pack higher and shifting his bow so it didn't rub against a shoulder blade. *I wonder if he saw Devas during his trial. I wonder if he—*

Ravan froze.

Hoofbeats coming down the road. From which direction? He couldn't tell. Desperately, he looked around as the clatter of the hoofs echoed closer. Trees hemmed him in from every side.

Off the road, off the road, off the road! With a hiss, he dove into the bush, scrambling behind the bole of a massive rosewood, catching his breath as he fell and rolled in.

His heartbeat roared in his ears, fingers afire on the string of his bow, thumb brushing the feathers of the arrow he had nocked.

He blinked. When had he nocked the arrow? *Get down, you fool!*

The thundering hooves grew closer, and abruptly, a file of horsemen swung into view. Devas. *Not slavers—proper warriors.* They wore chain-mail armour, iron helms and graceful sabres at their hips.

Tall and proud in the saddle, magnificent yet terrifying, their faces as hard and pitiless as the basket-hilted blades they wore. Then came the Kinnaras. Ravan had never seen so many of the half-Narakan, half-horse beings from the west. There were two dozen of them chained together by a running line ending in collars across their Narakan necks; half a dozen Devan warriors led them, and half a dozen followed behind, lashing them with whips and cursing in broken Samskritam.

The train did not end there. Instead, there came another six warriors and then a cluster of chained and beaten Kinnaras. And then another and yet another, on and on, in a seemingly endless line, until Ravan was sure they were hundreds strong. The Kinnaras were shockingly frail, their horse-hips jutting out like wings, ribs outlined in horrifying detail. They struggled to stay upright, and every time they slowed, their slavers whipped them without mercy. Judging from the amount of lather and blood running down the creatures' flanks, they'd been running hard for quite some time.

Ravan's blood began to boil. This time, his fear was much slower to give him pause. Before he realized it, he had edged forward from the rosewood and stretched back his dhanush, a mantra forming on his lips. *I can stop those Devas in their tracks!* Just one arrow, a spell of breaking, of falling. *Fell a massive shaala tree across the path and watch as the legs of the Devan horses snap like brittle twigs.*

I could shoot them through the throat and. . .

He found himself quivering, a maelstrom of emotion. Fear battled with hatred battled with wisdom battled with courage deep inside him. *Run!* His thumb brushed against the feathers, as it had a thousand times before. *Run, by Shiva's blood! There are dozens of them. I can't kill them all.*

The Kinnaras bled. Devan whips slashed through the air, and each stroke that landed was a cut upon his soul.

RUN! Ravan turned and fled. Bounding over shaala stumps and clustered limestone boulders, ducking beneath neem branches, slapping the vines out of the way, holding his dhanush close.

Calm. After a few minutes, Ravan slowed and stopped, looking around. Noticing a vine-shrouded ridge, he climbed it, and then leaped onto a broad branch of an ironwood tree. It jutted out sideways from the ridge, angled at just the right degree to offer a ramp.

Ravan whispered a balancing mantra and bounded up the branch with practiced ease.

The jungle canopy stretched out below him, a mantle of spreading green disrupted in the distance by the broad road slicing through the foliage.

He traced the road with his eyes as it wound off to the north. "North and south," he muttered, scanning the sky for the sun. *I came in from the east, and this runs north and south. . .*

There. As it approached a granite ridge, the path was no longer a simple ripple in the green. Ravan gasped. Past the ridge was a vast clearing. He studied the slopes of the hill around the clearing. Slopes stripped of all vegetation. *Bleak. Bare and desolate,* Ravan thought.

Massive faces of layered granite, broken by reddish-orange land thrust forth from the ground, scarred by the marks of Devan and Narakankind. Ladders, pulleys, and tiny forms of sentient beings clung to the sides, like so many minuscule ants.

All around them was the mine. An array of massive machines dotted the area, like twisted monsters of wood and metal and smoke. Shafts, pulleys, levers, and wheels worked by watermills, and by slaves turning huge metal wheels. The smell of burning coal wafted up to where he was perched, and his stomach twisted with disgust. Rough wooden towers protruded from the jungle floor in the periphery of the mine, manned by sentries whose halberd tips gleamed in the sunlight.

So that's what a Devan mine looks like.

These machines don't belong on my realm. The forlorn creatures he saw seemed pale imitations of Narakankind.

Ravan watched for a minute longer, fascinated but also repulsed by the spinning wheels, the billowing smoke, the flash of sparks, and the sudden whoosh of flames. *What are these machines? Furnaces of some sort? A blistering scar upon the aranya. They're working my people to death. Vijaata bastards!*

His people, and others. *All the races of Naraka.* He recalled how the tall old wretch in the slave train had cried out when whipped. *Rakshasan. Too light-skinned to be a southern Rakshasan. He was of the northern islands.*

Asuras and northern Rakshasas had fought five bitter wars to a detente in just as many decades a century earlier. *Father hates their king with a vengeance.* Yet the slave who had helped the falling wretch bore the *trishul* tattoo, an Asuran mark of Lord Shiva.

All the races of Naraka. What horrors do these unfortunates face, that they are ready to work alongside bitter enemies?

He scampered down, slipping through the brush until the road appeared. Then, following its route and staying parallel within the brush, he set off towards the south.

Towards the mine.

Making his way to the lip of the granite ridge, the Asuran prince peered down at the valley. It had been razed and partially excavated until it resembled a massive crater. A wall of sharpened ironwood stakes encircled the clearing, each as thick as a Rakshasa and every span as tall as the stone walls of Lanka. The Devas had constructed the wall upon a mound of earth a dozen feet tall and steep enough to challenge the most agile who might attempt to climb it.

There were wooden towers every bowshot's distance. The closest tower to him was manned by a Devan halberdier and three longbowmen.

This is quite the affluent enterprise, Ravan judged, taking in the reddish-orange island in a sea of green.

And this is only one they have hidden. How many more like this, are buried deep in the aranya or in other parts of Naraka? The Devan quarters were clustered against a wall in the distance, sturdy structures of wood and packed earth, complete with shuttered windows.

Workers were everywhere, pushing carts of reddish-yellow ore, manning slag-heap furnaces, pulling up and lowering large containers into a dozen shafts. Devan overseers with whips strutted around, shouting orders. The acrid smell of smoke from burning coal permeated the valley. *Iron.* An *ayas* mine. *So, this is why Narakans are forbidden to venture deep in the aranya upon pain of death. But wouldn't Vidyadharan pisachas flying overhead have discovered this mine by now? The Devas have probably used powerful Brahmaic white magic to ward off the entire mine from view, even from above!*

I wonder how deep the mine shafts go, Ravan mused, shifting to get a better vantage point. *It seems like they are. . .*

His thoughts trailed off as he noticed something—a faint disturbance in the foliage. It was surprisingly close, much closer than the palisade wall of the mining complex.

Ravan stiffened, peering harder. Initially, he saw nothing. *By Shiva, I could swear I saw something move.* A ripple in the fabric of the forest.

It could have been anything. The faintest shifting of a shaala branch in the wind. The quiver of an ironwood branch as a bird took flight. The. . .

The slither of a giant green serpent as it turned to stare directly at him. As its massive, forked tongue slipped forth to sample the air, sharp and blood-red even. The green viper was coiled around a teak branch and stared at him with unblinking eyes.

Ravan froze, desperately hoping that he hadn't been detected. Common pit vipers could detect heat, but certainly not over great distances. *Don't snakes have poor eyesight? The only creature who could have sensed me from this distance, hidden as I am, is. . .*

By the third eye of Shiva! He cast a mantra and stared, following the variegated black design on the viper's back. *This snake is bound! Scarcely visible leather straps tie it to the tree branch. It can only move its head around. It's powerless to move, or even coil.*

It came to him in a flash, and he rushed forward, bursting from the brush and reaching for his khukris.

The only creature that can detect me from this distance. . . a Naga! Captured by the Devas and used for its particular abilities. For its ability to unmask thermal signatures. For its ability to take a serpent's form. . .

He'd been spotted by a Naga and a prisoner of the Devas.

Guard me, O Shiva, Destroyer of Evil. His blades were heavy in his hands as he pumped forward towards the Naga, slashing through the brush with supernatural agility.

He was still too slow. He had spun a khukri to grasp it by the blade—just preparing for a desperate, full-speed throw at the Naga—when the giant viper lifted its head and tugged on something just above it.

A wire, whisper thin. There was a quiver of movement through the leaves, rippling to a nearby tower in the palisade. Then Ravan heard the resonant, powerful ringing of a bell, and everything exploded into chaos.

"*Akraamaka!*" The Devan sentries shouted. "Intruder!" One of them snatched a hammer and rang a gong. "Intruder at the eastern wall!" As the mine erupted into frenzied activity, Devas at guard towers now glowered in Ravan's direction.

I'm done for! His presence had been revealed; there was no helping that now. Abandoning all pretext of stealth, he turned and dashed down the ridge he'd painstakingly ascended.

"Open the gates!" A guard's voice roared behind him. "Sentry Nagas, at the ready! Unleash the Molossian hounds!"

Blood pounding through him, Ravan forgot his training. He ran with no other purpose than to flee, slamming through the brush with the blind madness of a wounded beast.

I'm dead. They'll find me, and they'll kill me. There are dozens of them, with dogs and Nagas and Brahmaic magic! What hope do I have against so many?

You are small as the leaf is small, his Teacher whispered. *As the ant is small. As the viper is small. Each in the way of its nature, the way of perfection.*

The only way to win was to *become* the jungle. To *merge* with the melodies of the forest when it suited him and *counter-weave* them when not.

This is my home. I can beat them.

Become the aranya. Be at home in its vastness. Merge with its melodies.

Come on, kushmanda! He cursed and pushed his body harder. *Think! This pack's slowing me down. This pack. . .*

Verbal abuse flowed from his pursuers like a torrent. The insistent baying of dogs rang out in the forest behind him. *They'll follow my scent.*

He twisted, yanking off his pack and bringing it around as he scrambled through the brush.

Water. . . water. . . water. . . Jala is the first key to losing trackers. Water and stone.

There has to be a source of jala for the mine.

THINK! Cursing, he snatched his water masaka from his pack and muttered a mantra to lock and magnify the scent that clung to its leather skin—

आवृतापि पुनस् तस्य गन्धः सर्वत्र गच्छति ।

(Though concealed, its scent goes everywhere.)

Water. . . water. . . water. . . He wasn't finding any *jala.* The barking drew closer. Quickly, he flung his masaka down a ravine, praying to Shiva it would tumble a long way. But he doubted it would fool the dogs.

Next was his pack, its smell more potent. He slammed it against a giant teak tree, repeating his incantation and magnifying his scent all over the leviathan. There was a shimmer of light, a ripple of power, and then he flung the pack as high as he could into the branches.

Now burdened only by khukris, bow, and quiver, Ravan hurried on.

The baying of the Molossian hounds drew ever closer. Ravan bounded down a ravine, tripped, and fell headlong on a hidden root, then slithered down a bank of rotting leaves.

Water. There it was, a pool fed by a waterfall that chuckled idly over a bank of perfect moss.

So idyllic.

Ravan raced up, leaped into the pool, swam up to the waterfall until it cascaded down on to his face. Once there, he splashed upstream a distance and made sure to wet the rocks, to break branches, to crumple low-reaching leaves along the way.

Then he bounded back downstream, leaped into the pool from the waterfall, and turned across to the far side. He reached as high as he could up the embankment, searching for a handhold in the boulders underneath. *Perfect.* Legs pistoning below and arms grasping ahead, he scrambled up the bank. His feet and hands gouged large chunks from the moss, dark and ragged stains that stood out like the hollow sockets of a giant skull.

When he reached the top, he didn't slow down, dashing across the greenish-brown earth with the frenzy of a madman. Branches snapped, leaves tore off before him, and a trail of upturned rot left patches of glistening moisture on the ground.

Rocks, rocks, rocks. After a few minutes, he slowed, seeing what he needed. Another ridge—of bare limestone shelves. He rushed over awkwardly, his trail clearly marked.

Then he turned back, away from the shelf. He hummed the Shanti mantra for peace, as his heartbeat stilled, and the heaving of his chest slowed. . .

> सर्वेशम् स्वस्तिर् भवतु। सर्वेशम् शन्तिर् भवतु।
> सर्वेशम् पुर्नम् भवतु। सर्वेशम् मन्गलम् भवतु।

> (May there be happiness in all; May there be peace in all May there be completeness in all; May there be success in all.)

Small as the leaf is small. As the ant is small. As the viper is small. Each in the way of its nature, the way of perfection. To merge with the melodies of the jungle.

He muttered an incantation to spread his scent upon the wind. He sensed it swirl up the ridge and dance along the limestone ledges. *To erase a thing with magic is sometimes possible but difficult,* the Teacher whispered. *Things do not just disappear; it's not the way of nature.* Not to dematerialize but to take a different form. A semblance of nonexistence.

Using spells one after the other left him feeling limp and faintly breathless.

Then came the trees. *I have time. The dogs are probably minutes away, even if the pack and masaka fail to confuse them.* He scaled the nearest teak with great effort and leaped from one branch to another, and then from one tree to another, until there was no easy trail to follow.

This will deceive the Devas. A false trail for them, and a false scent for their hounds.

He scampered down the last tree in the grove and ran in the direction of the stream he'd encountered before. He moved swiftly and smoothly, ephemeral as the wind. Ravan touched nothing and left nothing behind, and when he made it to the stream, he slid in, sleek as an otter.

Five minutes later, he emerged, quick but careful, trotting downstream, and then he found a trail—the same path he had taken to get to the road that led to the mine. Shaking his limbs of excess water and brushing the soil gently behind him with leaves to hide signs that he had ever been there, he walked backward for the first two hundred steps.

The barking of the dogs faded.

Shiva's trident. He shuddered. *That was close. The Devas are using venomous Nagas as heat-sensing sentries.* As Naraka's shapeshifting race, Nagas enjoyed the heightened abilities of many species. The durability, hearing, and keen vision of Rakshasas, the sensitivity to scents, and their serpent cousins' thermal detection. *The durability and stamina of a Rakshasa, the stealth and quickness of a snake. Magnified tenfold.*

It was hardly fair. Nagas came in two varieties, each equally terrifying: those who could transform into massive constrictors and those who could turn into adders, usually some form of pit viper.

The Devas were using the smaller, venomous variety as sentries for their higher sensitivity and the reduced likelihood that they'd be spotted. *Smaller than the constrictors but still giants to us Asurans!*

Clever. He shook his head, striding down the path, adjusting his quiver and khukris on his back and his bow in his left hand. The butterflies had not entirely fled his stomach. His abilities had been truly tested in the chaos of escape. He silently thanked his teachers for their prescience. For the prey he had hunted. The traps he had set. And the Asuras he had tracked.

But I've never had to flee for my life. Never had he looked in the eyes of warriors who wanted to kill him and turned to escape using magic and will.

My mind is sharp, and my veins thrum with vigour, but I know it will not last. Soon the lethargy would come. The weariness of after-magic.

I'll have to find safety, he thought, *replenish my food supply, and find a source of wa—*

Something slammed into him from behind, striking just between the shoulder blades. His chest rammed forward as if it had been pounded by a boulder. Everything happened in horrendous, bloodcurdling slow motion. His head snapped forward a heartbeat later as if suspended from a string. Ravan's arms pinwheeled in the air, and the bow flew from his hands. Arrows scattered from his quiver, and the breath sprang from his lungs in a *whoosh.*

The Devas couldn't have found me this quickly. And that's no Devan arrow.

Its momentum was far too strong to be anything Devan or Narakan-powered. Whoever had struck Ravan was riding a large horse or something even bigger.

There had been no warning. No sound. No vibration through the ground.

And then, the Asuran prince shuddered, flooded with sudden recognition.

Followed by horror.

I need my bow. Skidding across the damp ground, Ravan flailed desperately to turn around. To face a great being that reared above the prince with a feral roar.

Chapter 5

Once by Coil, Once by Fang, Once by Blade

Vaasuki slithered out of her family's nest in Nagan midform, half-Narakan and half-serpent, as quietly as she could. Her sister gave her cover by coughing so their sleeping father, tired from a long day of hunting, wouldn't hear her leave. It was time for her martial arts class with the Teacher, and it would be at least two hours before she arrived at the secret gurukul or training cavern where Ravan and she met the Teacher three times a week.

It required a bit more stealth to leave her tiny village of Sesha Madura, bordered on one side by the aranya, and on the other by the vast plain dominated by Devas with their stronghold at the Marut Castle. First, she had to avoid the vigil of the village night guards, all viper Nagas gifted with thermal vision. She did this by masking herself with a camouflage outfit her sister had stitched for her. Covered with leaves, twigs, and clumps of grass, she also smeared her entire body with mud from the banks of the stream that ran through her backyard. She was thermally invisible to the guards now, and inched her way to the fifteen-foot-tall wall of stakes that surrounded her border village.

Finally, Vaasuki reached the corner of the wall, where she had hidden her supplies. Picking up her arrows, her composite bow made with horn, wood, and sinew, as well as her bronze *dao* broadsword, she left her village. She made good time, avoiding the predators that roamed her route at night, and slid through a range of environments, from lush rainforest infested with howlers to sun-dried savannah to scrub forests. The trail regularly changed from rocky singletrack to well-worn footpaths used by locals, both Nagas and Asuras, mostly traders, as they travelled from village to village. As she arrived at the edge of the Simha aranya's boundary and entered, she saw the sign of the Teacher, a great *aum* on a massive teak tree. She uttered the magic phrase:

तेजस्विनावधीतमस्तु ।

(May our efforts at learning be luminous and filled with joy.)

A hidden door cut into the tree slid in, revealing a flight of descending steps. Ensuring that no one was watching, Vaasuki slithered down the stairs and into the main hall of the massive underground gurukul. The humongous cavern had many rooms linked with corridors, lit with blazing torches, none brighter than the charisma exhibited by the Teacher, who walked towards her.

"You're late," he said, smiling his characteristic smile. "Let's start with yoga stretches. Do ten surya namaskars, followed by *paripurna navasan*, working your abdominal muscles. Then, we'll do *dhanurasan*, followed by *setu bandh sarvangasan*. You know the sequence after that. . . "

"Yes, Teacher, I do; we've only done it a few thousand times," said Vaasuki, a wry grin forming on her lips. "*Balaasan, tittibhaasan, viraasan, salambhaasan, tadaasan, halaasan, padmaasan,* ending with shavaasan—the corpse."

The wise Master corrected her gently as she twisted herself into various poses, using her long tail for support, and stretching the different segments of her unique body to ready herself for the martial arts practice that would ensue.

An hour in, flushed with warmth, she was prepared for archery and sword fighting with her dao sword. She relished archery, the feeling of lining her body up perpendicular to the target. When she was ready to shoot, she was sure that she could draw an imaginary line from herself to the target, the line going across the first contact of her tail with the ground.

Vaasuki was left-eye dominant, so she held the bow with her right hand, pointing her left shoulder to the target, and handled the goose-feathered arrow and string with her right hand. Keeping her back erect, she adjusted her long tail until she was perfectly upright.

She pointed her composite bow down and nocked an arrow to the string.

With her fingers on the drawstring, she raised the bow and held it out towards the wood-and-straw target with circles and Samskritam symbols on it. Her focus was intense, on the centre of the target, and she released cleanly, her fingers relaxing as the arrow sped away from the bow towards its goal a hundred meters away. It hit the centre as the Teacher murmured, "Don't forget the recoil. . . "

However, his warning was well heeded, and Vaasuki stayed perfectly balanced, reloading with a new arrow for her next shot. After about an hour had passed, it was time for swordplay. Vaasuki changed into narakanform, preferring to duel with the flexibility her feet provided. The Teacher smiled once again as they put on their guards and thick rhinoceros-leather armour, and proceeded to spar. He picked up a Swargan bronze double-handed longsword with its thrusting ability and guarding capacity to match Vaasuki's double-handed dao, with its cutting ability, technical versatility, and durability. Vaasuki felt a sense of pride surge through her every time she picked up her dao; it was a gift from the Teacher when she won her first fight. A traditional weapon of her people, the long, squarish blade juxtaposed with an exquisite ivory hilt was perfectly balanced and carved with a scene from the famous Nagan saga called *Vritra's Prayer.* Forged by the Teacher himself, the dao was her prized possession; with the blade in hand, she felt invincible.

They held their respective swords, polished bronze gleaming in the lamplight, and brought them to their foreheads, a gesture of respect. The sensation was magical; the power of the dao coursed through her veins. She remembered the Teacher's words. *You have already lost the swordfight if you and your blade are two separate entities. Speak to the blade, but first, listen to it. Then, merge with it.*

One with the blade, she circled the Teacher. They scanned each other for a weak spot that could be exploited. After a few wary seconds, Vaasuki made the first move, striking out at the Teacher's torso with her dao. The Teacher blocked the attack gracefully, and the impact from the clash of the swords startled her.

She moved back a couple of paces to recover her balance. *Never mind,* she thought. *The element of surprise is of no use against him.* He could probably anticipate her next five moves. *I have to wait for him to strike, then react with a counterattack.* And so the two circled each other again.

Their feet moved in an unspoken yet shared rhythm and resembled a graceful dance.

The Teacher struck at Vaasuki's upper torso. As she raised her arms to block the strike, he quickly thrust his longsword towards Vaasuki's hip. Vaasuki leaped back, eyes wide and breath desperate. *If this were a duel, that would have been a fatal blow.*

Vaasuki was determined to prove her skill. She readjusted her grip on the dao and planted her feet firmly. The Teacher lunged forward but merely struck the blade collar of the dao. Vaasuki blocked the strike with agility and parried, her dao striking his longsword at the base of the weapon. The Master took a few steps back. Vaasuki thought she saw the hint of a smile on his typically serious face. For her, that was enough.

Rejuvenated with confidence, she held the dao high. The Teacher thrust his longsword at her head, and it met Vaasuki's dao at its edge. Vaasuki blocked the strike and immediately responded by striking at his torso. Her dao ended up meeting the longsword at its tip. The sound of blades clashing resonated through the gurukul.

Vaasuki noticed that the Teacher had moved away from his starting point while her feet had remained rooted to her spot. So, she chose to push him back, taking a giant step forward and striking out at him. Her dao was parried by his longsword, her blade meeting his at the longsword's ridge. Just as she predicted, the Teacher moved back to avoid the blow, and in the few seconds he took to regain his balance, Vaasuki struck again at the forte of the longsword. Her sharp blow weakened the Teacher's grip on his longsword, and Vaasuki beamed, realizing she'd broken the connection between the Teacher and his weapon.

I'm close to winning, but I haven't won yet. Heat flushed through her as Vaasuki knew that the next few moments of the match were crucial. She had succeeded in catching the Teacher off guard. As he strengthened his grip yet again, Vaasuki moved forward and rammed the square tip of her blade into the flat of the longsword. The force of the blow disarmed the Teacher, and when Vaasuki slid around and pointed the tip of her dao at his neck, their eyes met. *If this were a duel, that would have been a fatal blow.* Vaasuki slowly lowered the dao sword to her side, her stone-cold face betraying no sign of emotion, but when she looked at the Teacher's face and saw a smile, she couldn't help but smile too.

As Vaasuki finished her training regimen with stretches, she asked the Teacher, "Any word of Ravan?"

"No, my student, my dear *vidyarthi,* none. But I'm confident that he will face and beat whatever he encounters, Devan iron or predator claws."

That's curious, Vaasuki thought. *Why would Ravan encounter Devan warriors in the aranya of all places?* "The aranya is off-limits to all the races of Naraka; we Nagas have been warned of exile or worse if we venture in. . . Are you saying there might be Devas inside the deep jungle? What would they be doing so far from their strongholds at Maniraj-Khani, Kaanchana Giri, and Agni's castle on Ratnapur Island? Not to mention the Marut and Vayu castles!"

The Teacher sighed and began to tell Vaasuki what had festered in the aranya for generations, what the Devas had been doing to Narakans for centuries. . .

When he finished, his ward bowed to him deeply. Eyes blazing, she declared, "How dare the Devas desecrate Vritra's Breath thus! Give us the order on what we should do, Ravan and me. We will carry out your command with every vestige of skill you have imparted to us, and with every *pala,* every ounce of strength. With every ounce of cunning and by the power of the magic we have learned. By the power of the four Vedas! The Devas will pay the price for what they have done to Naraka, by Vritra's tomb. . . "

Chapter 6

Water, Fire, Needle

Ravan had two advantages over the thing that had attacked him.

He had the magic of the four Vedas. He had trained from the age of five in the spells and enchantments of the first three—*Rig, Yajur, and Sama*—under Shukra. Only a handful of Narakans received that gift, mostly highborn Asuras. The dark arts of the *Atharva,* he and Vaasuki had laboured over under the Teacher. *Thank you for bringing me to the Teacher, Matr!*

Head still ringing from the impact of the blow, Ravan shouted a mantra of binding.

सप्त गुरुप्रसादेन; यदा जागरतिकुण्डलिनी |
तदा सर्वानिपद्मानि;व्यदित्यन्त्ते घ्रन्थयोऽपिच ||

(When the grace of the Teacher arouses the dormant Kundalini,
then alone, all the chakras are opened and
the knots of the target are bound. . .)

His spell caught the creature's roar and spun it about, weaving it through the aam trees, shaking their branches with its power. The preternatural force of the spell shook the forest floor.

A potent wind charged with magic rushed through the clearing, and the creature backed away in hesitation. *This thing is not natural,* the wind said. *This prey is protected.*

And then, there was Ravan's second advantage. Nature had armed his attacker with an exquisite set of weapons and with senses tuned to hunting. But it was a brute in the end.

That was why, as he lay sprawled in the dust, as the agony of injury and the fire of determination swirled through his mind in numbing tandem, the creature hesitated in its charge. Instead, the massive beast reared up and roared its presence to the skies.

This realm is mine, the roar said. *All shall know my dominion over it.*

It was a classic display of dominance, and it gave Ravan the time he needed to roll frantically over to his bow and to look up.

His mind fractured into a thousand thoughts as he gawked at the monster.

A giant lion's body, muscles coiled and powerful beneath the massive wings of an eagle. Feathers that gleamed as if recently burnished by a coppersmith. It was larger than a Devan draft horse. *Its supernatural mass and power come from Devan Brahmaic magic.*

The Asuran prince gaped at jagged bloodstained fangs, at amber eyes alight with a savage fury.

Simurgh. Shiva's blade. I disturbed a simurgh at its meal. It will show me no quarter.

No one knew how the feared monsters had come to be on Naraka. Asuran lore painted them as one of the aranya's nightmarish impossibilities. Ancient products, it was believed, of occult experimentation by the Gods. The Vidyadharas actually thought the winged beings to *be* Gods, descended to live among narakankind, to revel in the enormity of their power.

The *simurgh* let loose another roar and dropped to all fours, lips lifted in a bloody snarl. Slowly, it paced the jungle floor, wings folded and tail swishing back and forth, indicating an imminent charge.

But it sensed danger from Ravan, and it paused.

This is a dangerous, magical being.

Ravan's hand found an arrow in the dust. He nocked it with practised speed as he twisted up to a half-crouch, half-kneel, bow swinging around as he drew the bronze-tipped arrow. A primal growl rippled from the beast's throat as it crouched, coiled, and sprang. *It's too quick; I can't make the shot in time.*

In desperation, he dove low to the ground, lunging to undercut the simurgh's leap. Its jaws barely missed his throat, but its foreclaws reached out, slashed his back, and lay it open as the Asuran prince crashed on to the jungle floor.

Ravan screamed in agony as the giant claws sliced cleanly through his flesh. With great effort, he gritted his teeth and spun his body, the beast right on top of him. One of his khukris nearly slipped out of his right hand. *When did I draw it?* He still held the dhanush in his left hand, but the arrowhead had snapped against the ground.

Desperately, the prince lunged into the mass of the demon as it turned. Its claws raked at him, fangs snicking down, but his lunge was unexpected. The simurgh's teeth missed him again as Ravan tucked his head down and rammed his khukri up between its forelegs. Its claws missed his vitals but tore nasty, bloody furrows from shoulders to ribs.

Still, Ravan got in a crucial blow. *"Vijaata. . . bastard!"* he screamed, plunging a bronze khukri deep into the softness just beneath the creature's left shoulder. The simurgh roared and flung him off, retreating with a snarl.

Ravan's curved blade lay buried in the monster's breast, all the way to the hilt. A maniacal laugh escaped his lips. He'd struck a rib, but the entire fifteen inches of his blade had pierced through flesh and muscle. *It'll lose blood fast.*

As for him, the pain would come. But not just yet. *I have seconds before I lose consciousness. Go!*

He shouted a mantra to stop the creature in its tracks. . .

ओ शिव! मुर्ना म्रुगस्य दन्त अपिशीर्णापृष्टयः |
निर्मुक्ते गोधा भवतु नीचायच्छशयुर्मृगः ||

(By nearest way let him be gone! Let Shiva slay him with his bolt!
Let the beast's teeth be broken off, sinews shivered, and shattered be his ribs!)

The creature stopped. It crouched, snarling, signalling a charge. Ravan screamed and stumbled forward, flailing his arms. The monster retreated in doubt. "I can sting you!" he shrieked. "Fear me!" *I just need a moment, a heartbeat, the time to stoop and—*

There. Snatching a fallen arrow from the ground, he nocked and drew in a sinuous move of anguish. The wounds on his back and chest opened as he strained, injured muscles unknotting, blood spraying on to the jungle floor.

But he stood firm and drew.

Ravan was the finest archer in all Asurapura. He had trained two hours every day since the age of five. He could hit a coin tossed from a balcony at a hundred paces nine times out of ten. The goose-feathered shaft took the monster in the eye as its hind legs left the ground, burying itself deep in the creature's brain. But the simurgh had momentum, and Ravan was too weak to avoid its outstretched foreclaws.

But they had no life in them. The beast's body struck him with the momentum of a runaway cart and sent him sprawling, but then, with a great sigh, the monster breathed its last.

The prince stepped back from the dead animal, his breath coming in laboured gasps. The sounds of the jungle entered his ears through a wall of numbness. His legs quivered beneath him, and he stumbled, falling to his knees.

Have to find water, fire, needle. I've been wounded before and survived. But he couldn't remember being in a worse state.

Memories flooded his brain. *That time the Teacher sent me out from camp alone, to hunt boar.* He'd failed, thigh lacerated to the bone by the sharp tusks of the beast. Bleeding profusely, he'd dragged himself step by tortured step through the jungle, before collapsing at his Teacher's feet.

The wise one gave him a scolding for the failed hunt—then another for abusing his wound. *Never take a step until you've seen to an injury like that,* the Teacher had snapped. Then, he'd used water, fire, and a needle to clean and stitch Ravan's wound with expert hands.

When you fail but survive, Asuran Prince, then you're on the path to becoming a King, the Teacher had said. It had stung at the time. *I couldn't have defeated the simurgh without your lessons,* he thought fiercely. *Never again will I doubt your wisdom.*

Water, fire, needle. He looked down at his hands. They were dark and wet with blood; crimson droplets splattered from his fingers, creating a small pool upon the trail. *The trail. I have to get the simurgh off the path. If the Devas come, they'll see the body. . .*

Stumbling forward, he flung aside his bow.

Water. Fire. Needle. He staggered towards the creature, reaching for the bronze khukri that lay embedded in its body. Several minutes elapsed before he managed to draw the knife from the corpse and kneel at the beast's side. His arrow protruded from the gory eye of the lion-faced beast, white-ribbed goose feathers blurring momentarily before snapping back into focus.

His body was a throbbing mass of agony. A dozen lacerations on his shoulders, back, and ribs wept dark blood. *I'm fading. Don't have much strength. Losing too much blood.* The aranya blurred around him, blues of the sky mingling with the green foliage and the gold and red of the devil he'd conquered. *My wounds. . .*

He swayed and nearly stumbled, a peculiar smile forming on his face as the jungle danced around him. Ravan's mind flooded with memories of his pitr twirling him around as a boy. Grabbing him by the hands, spinning him round and round. A blur of dizzying, disorienting madness.

Cursing, he slapped his thigh, muttering the mantra of immortality to his Lord. . .

> ॐ त्र्यंम्बकं यजामहे सुगन्धिं पुष्टिवर्धनम् ।
> उर्वारुकमिंव बन्धंनान् मृत्योर्मुक्षीय मा ऽमृतांत् । ।

> (We worship Shiva—the Three-Eyed Lord—who is fragrant, nourishes, and grows all beings.

As the ripened cucumber is liberated by the farmer from its bondage to the vine when it fully ripens, may He liberate us from death and lead us to immortality.)

Chapter 7

Spawn of a Monster

Day Six

Ravan awoke to fire. It covered his back, wrapped around his sides, and shrieked agony when he tried to move.

Twilight approaches, he thought. But a few narrow beams of light still filtered in through the soaring canopy. *When did I secure my pack? And when did I wash and sew up my wounds?*

His senses trickled back like wheat through a brass sieve in Lanka's kitchens. Slowly, he sat up, wincing and then groaning aloud at the pain that wracked his body.

The prince's hands splayed across the wet grass as he braced himself upright. The banana leaves that covered him shifted off him further.

He frowned. Something was wrong. The light. . . The grass. . .

Ravan hissed in sudden realization, lifting his palms for inspection.

Wet *kusha* grass. *Dew.*

It's dawn, not twilight, he realized in horror, glancing wildly about a thicket of mulberry shrubs. *I've slept a whole night and a day.*

He was coated in the poisonous white sap of the mulberry and with mud. Half-buried, deep in a cycad, his masaka by his side. *My masaka! Did Lord Shiva himself bring it back to me? Am I protected by Him? Or did I go back for it last night? Across the stream, back in the direction of the mine?*

He'd done an excellent job of hiding himself and masking his scent. Nevertheless, he was lucky to be alive. *Passing a night unscathed in the aranya while wounded and unconscious is nothing to sneer at.* He cast a spell to keep the ants, mosquitoes, and poisonous arachnids away for the day.

Despite the pain, Ravan levered himself up on his knees, and twisting his neck, inspected his work. *Thank you, Teacher, for teaching us the suturing arts. The immortality mantra must have somehow sustained me until I cleaned and sewed up my wound.* The bandages were tight but breathed and felt clean of blood or pus. On the inside, he felt the fresh, moist bulge of a poultice.

On his lower back, there was a warmth where the deepest wounds had split open. *I should close those up as soon as possible.*

But first, I have to get out of the aranya. The Devas were likely nearby; scavengers had undoubtedly been at the simurgh's body by now, and he was lucky he hadn't been attacked while he slept.

The minutes that followed were a nightmare. Ravan battled out of the cycad's thorns, and stumbling through the trees, he somehow found the Devan trail that led to the mine. The aranya was a dangerous place: vipers, howler monkeys, leopards, hyenas, even lions.

He took stock. *Am I lucid? Is my mind dancing on the cusp of hallucination? Am I leaving a trail or making too much noise?*

His every sense strained, seeking a way out. He did the morning *vandana* ritual with the few drops of water left in the masaka. *If I ever make it back, a full recovery will take time.*

Can I secure any meat off the simurgh? he thought desperately. *Maybe there's something left.* He had everything he needed to start a fire, cook a meal. *I should have done that last night. But then, I barely sewed up the worst of my wounds before collapsing.*

He stumbled forward on the trail, leaning on his bow like a crippled warrior floundering in Kaala's halls of death. The sun was bright and the wind gentle, and for a moment, he stood swaying on the path, basking in the warmth.

"Have to move," he hissed. "Have to get to the creature's body, then to Lanka." *How far away am I, straight walking? Three days? Two?*

"No," he muttered. It would be suicide to try such a thing in his condition. *Better to sleep, to eat, to regain my vigour first.*

I won't make it back in seven days. My realm, Asurapura, will think I died. My family will think I failed the Trial of Seven Days. Father's disgust. . .

The smell assailed him before the massive body came into view—a noxious, sulphurous odour. Something had torn the belly of the simurgh open, spilling its insides out on the path. A committee of king vultures squabbled over the guts a short way off. The monster's breasts were gone, large chunks of meat shredded off the ribs, but there was still a haunch intact, twisted back from the pelvis at an awkward angle.

He eased himself closer with the bow, breath ragged. Despite their name, king vultures were cowards; they wouldn't be a problem. *I'll take as much meat as I can carry and maybe a tooth for remembrance. A tooth or a claw, yes. That would make a right imposing necklace.*

Ravan snorted, picking up his quiver and arrows from the ground. He was brave, the way he'd spied on the Devas, infiltrating their mine, and then evading their molossi hounds with magic.

But in my foolhardiness, I ignored the signs. Ran right into the hunting grounds of a thrice-damned simurgh, by Shiva's trident, and. . .

From within the cluster of vultures, something wailed. The vultures scrambled backward in a flurry of feathers, hissing and grunting in alarm.

It screeched again, whatever it was, and Ravan saw the flash of a beleaguered head inside the simurgh's mass, its teeth snapping as it struggled. It was a cat's head, and a tiny one at that. *Like the felines that roam Chandra Rajakula palace. . .*

"Shiva's blood!" he cursed, stumbling into a run. "Get away! Get away, you vijaatas. Bastards!" And then he attacked the creatures, flailing wildly with his bow. His shoulders shrieked in agony; hot wetness broke out upon his back. "Get away!" With a chorus of resentful cries, the vultures took to the sky, flapping laboriously up and then wheeled smoothly to land a dozen feet away. One of them, particularly bold, waddled forward and snapped at the tiny animal one more time.

"BACK!" Ravan howled, hurling his dhanush. It struck the creature a glancing blow and sent it dashing away with a shriek.

"A baby!" Ravan stared in disbelief. "A simurgh baby?" The tiny thing whimpered, skipped back, and retreated to the lifeless body of its mother. It pawed her face in distress and wailed, then whirled and spat a vicious hiss at the young Asura.

"That's ok," Ravan murmured, "I won't hurt you." *I killed your mother, true, but I won't hurt you.* He bent carefully to retrieve his bow and saw the baby tense as he lowered himself, squatting down at its level.

The tiny beast was frightened, but tilting its head, it gave him a curious sideways glance. Tentatively, he extended a hand, cooing softly as with the palace cats. *You must have hidden nearby, maybe in your mother's den? You're lucky, little one, that you didn't come back to your mother until I returned. Otherwise, the vultures would have. . .*

An unexpectedly long tail swished anxiously behind the creature as it huddled closer to the head of its dead mother.

"You're pretty, aren't you?" For a moment, Ravan's wounds didn't bother him. Blood seeped through the bandages on his back, dribbling towards the muddied earth below, but he didn't flinch. Simurghs were all over the palace in mosaic and paintings and carved into the legs of thrones. Father even had one stuffed behind his seat in the hall of private audience or Mantrana Aasthaana.

You're a real beauty. Its feathers were a deep and burnished gold, as was its head, its forelegs, and tail. Its eyes were a liquid amber, burning from within. The mane had not yet begun to form, but he saw from its tiny manhood that it was male. *Did simurghs have to undergo trials to become twice-born?*

The courage of a twice-born, a dvija. That's what I need now before the jungle kills us both.

"I won't hurt you," he repeated, lowering his bow to the earth. The vultures gathered and bustled closer, squawking a warning. Ravan eyed them thoughtfully, hand drifting towards his quiver.

They didn't respond, other than to shoot him a wary glance.

Through some stroke of fortune long due, his shot took two of them at once. It went clean through the first's neck and pierced the side of the next, skewering them together as neatly as *bhaditrakam. Meat grilled on a skewer. A snack favoured by Kinnaras.*

Sighing, Ravan hastened over to put the birds out of their misery, his khukris flashing in the morning light.

"But no more," he warned the baby, probing his shoulder ruefully with a finger as he brought the bodies of the vultures over. "Another shot like that and my back will break open and I'll bleed to death."

The creature regarded him for a moment, then meowed pitifully, as if to say it hadn't agreed to any of this.

"Oh, you're coming with me," Ravan chuckled as he gutted and dressed two of the vultures. "I've killed your mother, and you'll die if I leave you out here. Can't have both of you weighing on my soul. One endangered and mythical dead creature is enough." As he stuffed the birds into his pack after airing them for a bit, his thoughts wandered.

I'm not lucid. There's a tinge of fever touching upon my mind. Still, I have enough rajas, or inner fire, holding me up for now.

It took a while to draw the baby simurgh away from its mother's lifeless body. It broke his heart to do so.

"Don't know why I'm even doing this," he grumbled, trekking down the trail as the hours passed. The smell of vulture had finally coaxed the thing away, but he'd lost precious time. *I can't believe I'm risking my neck and bleeding my life out for the spawn of a monster that tried to kill me.*

Still, there was something magical, something precious about the creature that peered out over the top of his pack. The pack weighed heavily on his wounds, but they would need the vulture meat. *I'll save this baby, come what may!*

Unfortunately, he was unable to secure much by way of other fresh food. After gathering a few mangos from the trees, he shot a couple of curious squirrels that had arrived to investigate.

Still, there was a touch of fortune in his encounter with the mother. Her scent had melded with his during her final battle, and now he was the last living creature whose smell and presence the little one trusted. *He's imprinted on me, just as a mother imprints on her baby.*

Progress was torturous. After several hours of struggling through the jungle, Ravan found a small stream. Making a fire, he boiled some water, then replaced the poultices and re-bandaged his wounds with clean linen from his miraculous masaka. *How did the pack appear from where I discarded it? Did Shiva himself bring it to me?*

One of the slashes on his back needed restitching with the heated three-pointed *tryasta* needle and linen thread, a difficult duty to perform on oneself. He managed with patience and flexibility, applying *vibhuti* on his back before the sun reached its zenith. Then, he set out once again.

The baby simurgh was a welcome if infuriating distraction from his pain. After a spell of petrified silence, it began whimpering softly, squirming in the pack and yowling to be set free. Sighing, Ravan began to offer scraps of vulture meat back over his shoulder. It snapped them up as Surpanakha did with sweetmeats, meowing for more.

"No," he growled finally, snatching the meat away. "Make noise, and you starve." The creature seemed to relent in the hours that followed.

As Ravan settled down to sleep that night after sandhya vandana prayers, he saw the baby didn't struggle to escape. Of course, he had tied its forepaws to his pack just to make sure.

He cast the usual spells to ward off insects and predators, set his mind inwards, and dozed off, haunted by dreams of half-Devan, half-eagle demons chasing him through the night. When they triumphed in their hunt, however, it wasn't him they caught and tortured. It was a small simurgh, orphaned by

Ravan's carelessness, pleading with innocent dying whimpers for him to rescue it.

Day Seven

As prince and baby simurgh trudged through the dense jungle, progress was slow. The prince's back was a throbbing plane of orchestrated agony, almost artistic in its expression. With every step he took, a ripple began at his lower back, rolling up from his sacrum and through every vertebra to crescendo at his neck. *Is it taking the path of kundalini during meditation?* The spasm seemed to last as long as it took Surpanakha to play an entire raga with her veena. And the little simurgh added to his misery by sinking its tiny claws into his shoulder. As it shifted around, its hooks sought purchase on him, and another wave of pain ensued.

He decided to count its presence as a blessing, and after padding the shoulder with another poultice and a linen bandage, he allowed it the perch. The little creature yowled from time to time. *Does it yearn for its mother?* As time passed, the little one progressed from a sulking silence to repeated growls. *The poor thing must be hungry.* Finally, it began to lick his cheek, meowing softly. *Is that affection, or a tactic to get food?* Ravan resolved to see him fully grown, healthy, and strong.

What will Pitr say to my bringing a beast of legend into the palace? He discarded the concern and hobbled on, content with the fact that no one, not even Su-Janghi Deathsinger, great Vidyadharan guru of pisacha training, had succeeded in raising a simurgh in captivity.

"We'll just have to succeed, won't we?" he asked his companion, tickling it under the chin. It meowed good-naturedly and nuzzled his head, whiskers tickling his ear.

The journey was a blur, a mélange of sights, sounds, and vague impressions. Greens of the jungle, browns of the trail, the cutting blue of the sky, calls of the purple-faced *langurs* and *bulbuls* as he searched the horizon for familiar markers. The heat and wetness of the steamy undergrowth, the jarring cacophony of the blue mynahs and howlers. Pugmarks of leopards that warned him away and untrammelled paths that gave him comfort. The whispery sliding of scales on the tree trunks, of serpents watching. Disappearing when he turned and shouted but always watching.

They sense my weakness yet fear me. Especially the vipers. They seem to have an instinct about us that even the ball python constrictors lack.

After his evening prayers to the Sun Elemental and Lord Shiva, the Asuran prince walked a time into the night, using a spell for light, assuring himself that he could stay alert. The first time, a large pit viper startled him, rustling through the undergrowth, he grumbled and kept on. The second time, it was a small leopard, and this time, he cursed and set about finding a tree where he and his tiny companion would be safe from predators. Covering himself with thunbergia vine and the sap of some strychnos leaves, sure to put off leopards or tigers, Ravan cast a protection mantra over himself and the little simurgh and slept a deep, dreamless sleep.

Day Eight

The next day passed much the same. *This tiny, magical creature's companionship keeps me alive.* The *tunnasevani,* or zigzag stitches, made by his three-pointed needle held. Sushruta's medical tome, *The Art of Suturing,* as taught by Shukra in his monotone had done the trick. Mercifully, the bleeding on his chest had stopped. But two slashes along his back and one along his flank had begun to fester. It was sheer torture to strip off the linen bandages, clean the wounds, boil the cloth strips, and wrap them on again. His head spun, and the realm swam before his eyes: the only thing that kept him going was the creature in his backpack, tiny and hungry, with its piteous cries.

His every movement was a long *ragamalika* of sheer agony. He began to think he wouldn't mind dying after all. Was being twice-born *that* important? Not if he had just himself to consider.

But my family? The helpless simurgh baby in my backpack? "For them, I will live," he swore. *What about Pitr's expectations?* The familiar voice in his head again. . .

"The Teacher said something about that once," he muttered, staring at the thing that curled in his lap as they settled in for the night after his prayers. "He said you find strength by pouring yourself out into others. In bleeding for the people you love." Ravan smiled wanly. "You're not a proper Asura, I suppose. But I will care for you, I swear." *I killed your mother. I might have left you to die. It's a miracle you're alive at all.* He jabbed the chital that cooked over his evening fire with a stick and brooded.

If life in a gilded cage in the palace can even be called a life for a free, wild being. Snatched from your mother, from the jungle where your kind have lived since the time of the prajapatis and their experiments. Forced to live in a palace, and with whom? Kumbhakarna's mudhol dogs? Mother's cats? Father's birds of prey? Raising a wild simurgh was going to be a challenge.

Day Nine

They took two wrong turns and lost nearly three hours circumventing a colossal granite ridge the next morning. Ravan could hardly put one foot before the other without cracking his wounds open. By himself, there was no way in Kaala's name that he would have scaled those boulders—but *they* were able to do it. They made it to the Fourteenth Peak by sundown, and now he was reasonably oriented.

"We'll cut across this valley in the morning," he told the creature that sat ensconced on his lap, pointing north, "and circle that lake at the other end. There should be some banded barb fish there, maybe a *sheat* catfish or two—easy fishing." He winced as the creature shifted, driving fire up his ribs. "I know it's slower, but we can't use the route I took into the aranya. Too many Devas. And now they know I know about their iron mine. . . " *Are they hunting me still? Enraged that a free Narakan noble had stumbled across their mines? Do they know who I am? Will they come to Lanka and demand my head?*

"Maybe it's best not to say anything about the mine," he muttered, peering off into the darkness. It was dark that night, the stars obscured by pregnant clouds. *The torrents of rain will soon come.*

"You need a name," he said, picking it up and knuckling the creature's bony head. It meowed pitifully and nuzzled closer to him, a low purr emanating from its chest.

"What's your name?" Pensively, he traced the curve of its jaw. *How could a creature lose its mother and sleep soundly the very next night?*

How can you sleep soundly at all? he wondered, glancing nervously at the tall dipterocarps around him. He usually slept without worry when alone. Burdened with the responsibility of his new charge, however, he slept fitfully.

"Maybe your name is 'He who is calm in the storm'?" *Sthitha-Pragyan.* He smiled softly, listening to the creature's happy purring. "A name that means trust. How can you trust me to keep you safe? We're both of us still younglings, and this aranya isn't even my home." *And I'm taking you out of yours.* "A name that has something to do with the jungle, then?" Mantras rolled around in his mind, his consciousness extended through the jungle, yet he couldn't rest. The creature was a tiny flame of life, and he held it cupped between his fingers, sheltered from the wind.

One twitch and he might crush the poor thing.

"Flame," he whispered, staring at the creature's hooded eyes. "Your feathers are flame in the sunlight; your eyes are flame at night. You're weak but not helpless. I will help you, and you'll grow strong and skilled. And one day, you'll become a bonfire. . . Hmmm, no. Not fire. Too common. Aah! Yes—you shall be Sharabha, the mighty incarnation of Lord Shiva that battled Goddess Pratyangira herself. You were sent to me by Aadideva, first among Gods. Without question, you have saved my life."

He snuggled deeper beneath the banyan they had chosen for their nocturnal shelter. Its broad, drooping branches and leaves promised refuge from the impending rain.

I wonder when we'll get home, Ravan thought, bowing his head and forcing his eyes closed. *I wonder if my kin and family have stopped the nightly vigil.* It was customary for a twice-born to return at sundown on the seventh day. Surviving at least seven days was paramount to being twice-born. Still, a morning arrival on the seventh day meant the Trial had been easy. It was seen as cowardly, a sign that you had evaded the great dangers of the jungle.

Traditional nonsense—most twice-born Asuras just waited at the forest's edge till sundown on the seventh, then emerged—but in Ravan's situation, it wouldn't matter. He'd be another three days at least, if not more. Eleven days in all, emerging on the twelfth. *If I ever get back to Lanka,* he thought, grimacing as his shoulder throbbed with pain.

Still, I'm glad to have a new friend deep in this pitiless aranya.

Chapter 8

If I'm to Love You Truly

Day Eleven

"Beautiful." Harsha's eyes scanned the horizon. "See how the Sun Elemental bleeds out as he rides across the sky? Not only across the clouds but over the jungle canopy itself? See how he gilds all with a golden fire? He swells up, peaks, and is gone."

Surpanakha's thoughts were elsewhere. *It's been ten whole days since the start of the Trial. And the eleventh swiftly draws to a close.*

They stood on the Sumukha Nivaasa level of the seven-level Chandra Rajakula Palace as the sun set upon the far range. At a trabeated window, whose frame was exquisitely adorned with blue tiles and gold engravings. Surpanakha adored the Sumukha, the Hall of Mirrors in the *yuvaraaja's* residence. Not quite as ornate as the Shaanti Nivaasa or the Shobha Nivaasa. But it was the only level in the Chandra Rajakula that made her feel at peace. *Pitr used to bring me here as a little girl. That's why I come here with my priyatama, my beloved, when Ravan is away. I feel safe here.*

The Sun Elemental. Swelling up. Peaking. And then, disappearing. The Asuran princess knew that Ravan would not return that day. For an instant, she thought she saw him—dark, curly locks bound back for unrestricted vision, bow bouncing across a shoulder as he strode. He walked with an adult's stride, swaggering and full of verve, out from the jungle that watched with its many eyes.

She envisioned it, prayed to Shiva that it be true. Just as she had done for several evenings, but her brother had not returned. Upon the eighth day, her prayers were frantic. Upon the ninth, they became trembling challenges thrown at Shiva, his consort Parvati, and even their divine children, Ganesha and Murugan.

The jungle just sat and murmured its ageless song.

"You know, if you think about it," Harsha said, "the sunrise never really ends, does it? Just one endless arc of twilight skimming across our realm. A single breath of beauty caught upon night's et—"

"Harsha!" *The poor boy's trying to comfort me. It's not working.*

"Surpanakha!" he burst out. "It cuts my soul to see you so depressed! It—"

"Cuts *your* soul?" she said. "By Shiva's third eye, he's my *brother*, Harsha. He's *my bhratr*, and it cuts *your* soul? Speaking of cut, have you considered that he might be somewhere on the jungle floor right now, a thousand ribbons of flesh sliced off his body? The leopards could—"

"Surpanakha." Harsha interrupted with compassion in his voice. "Dearest, I feel the fire that eats away at you. I, too, ache every moment he does not return. Look at me." moved and clasped her face with his hands, thumbs wiping away great tears that spilled down her cheeks. "Look at me. Ravan will make it back," he said in Samskritam, the tongue of the Gods. The language of Asuran priests. To say something in the Sacred Tongue meant you believed it truly.

And again, "Ravan will make it back."

Surpanakha sniffed and dried her eyes, burrowing her head into his chest. A muscular, well-veined arm encircled her, holding her tight.

"If he does not come tomorrow? And not for another ten days?" she asked.

Harsha sighed. "What can we do but wait?" He paused. "And pray to Shiva and Shakti?"

"What, indeed. . . " Surpanakha nodded pensively. Her gaze roved the jungle's sharp edge.

"Ohhh, no." He shifted, pulling her closer and forcing her face up to his own. "Ohhh, no, Surpanakha. Please tell me you don't mean to."

"You know me, *priyatama*," she said, pulling away and meeting his gaze. "Do you think you can dissuade me?"

"Surpanakha, come now!" Harsha tried to hug her closer, but she pushed him aside and scrambled to her feet, staring down in disapproval. "Surpanakha, you know it would be suicide!"

"Where is my Vidyadharan warrior?" she asked, jerking a quivering finger down the hill on which the palace stood, down to the wall of the brooding jungle. "Where is the fearless one who saw my inner fire and fell in love with it?"

She saw him flinch but didn't care. *My brother is out there in the treacherous aranya. Four days past his due. Mother sits in her chambers, too distraught to even go to the temple. Father. . .*

Father, she thought with a sneer, *wouldn't acknowledge his jyeshta putr's death, until the pyres had burned away every inch of Ravan's body. Pitr, with his concubines and his wars. And now Harsha dares tell me that chasing after Ravan will be suicide.*

She gazed out at the majestic, sweeping view of the aranya from the Hall of Mirrors.

Harsha's immense pisacha, Uluka, stirred and stretched, massive wingspan hardly concealed, on a tall dipterocarp nearby. The dragon cracked open an amber eye to peer at the young couple as they argued. The movement brought Surpanakha back to reality.

"Where is the courageous one who bravely climbed Bhavani temple's Thrice-Tall Spire in the Peaks?" she exclaimed. "The one who snatched me from the teeth of Asuran power on the wings of Uluka and whisked me away to the Peaks? Who defies his Goddess for love, who spits in the face of Kaala, of Death himself, for his priyatama?"

"Surpanakha," he breathed, eyes wide. "You are not yourself. Please, listen and remember—"

"Ravan said he'd come back!" she screamed, dashing down marble stairs towards the Shanti Nivaasa, the Hall of Rest. "Do you not trust he will return?" she wept, tears of burning anguish cascading down her beautiful round face. Her *katar* knife was on her hip, bow in hand. *When did I pick it up? No matter. It will be enough. I will find bhratr and—*

"Surpanakha!" Strong fingers caught her elbow, spinning her around. "I feel you, Surpanakha!" Tears coursed down his face.

How dare you cry? she thought.

"I love you, and that's exactly why you must listen! I turned away every princess whose family proposed marriage, disregarded my father's wishes, spurned the honour of my people to be with you." His eyes softened, and he edged closer, reaching out his lean, tanned arm. "You know my life is yours, Surpanakha. You know I love you with every fibre of my being. So listen, then, when I say that. . . Surpanakha?"

Oh, Gods. Oh, Shakti, Goddess of all realms. "Harsha," she sobbed weakly, crumpling to the brilliant, blue-tiled floor of the Shanti

Nivaasa. She'd instructed her ladies-in-waiting to keep the guards at bay. The tiles shone beneath, her priyatama's hands hot around her slender body. "Harsha, I don't hear anything. The jungle is completely silent. It doesn't speak to me, no matter how many raga-mantra spells I cast. It tells me nothing of Ravan's fate." *The aranya is as silent as great-uncle Suka Asura's meditation cave.*

"I'm sorry," she wept, covering her face and battling for breath.

"That's ok," he murmured. "That's alright, Surpanakha. My love, you are alright." Harsha's strong hands encircled her from behind and tugged her down, curling her up against his body. He cupped her as an outer floral covering protects the bud, wrapping her in his safe arms. "That's ok."

"Our silly laws sent him off to die!" she spat. "Pitr is so busy with his stupid Nagan war. Kumbhakarna won't even come to be with us, and Mother's not eating, and Ravan's. . . " Her body quivered as she sobbed, burying her face in her curled knees. "Ravan's not back, Harsha."

"I know. I know." He smoothed her lustrous black hair, voice warm against her ear. "But Kumbhakarna loves him. They all do. Kumbhakarna has his way of facing emotions, and you have yours."

"Yes!" she growled. "Except, Kumbhakarna's is throwing himself at his studies. He's picked up a strange martial art named kalarippayattu from a Rakshasan servant and practises the forms until he fades. My way of dealing with my emotions is action! I want to go into the aranya and save Ravan! High Priest Shukra will condemn it, and Mother will never allow it."

"So. . . " He paused. "We'll just have to do it so they don't know, eh?"

She blinked. Her trembling softened. "What did you say?"

He sighed. "I will help you, Surpanakha. We will go into the aranya."

"What? You. . . " She pushed away. *Your eyes! Priyatama, your eyes are full of the fire of conviction.* "You will?"

The Vidyadharan prince attempted a smile, razor-thin.

"But why? Just a moment ago, you—" Surpanakha started.

"Just a moment ago, I thought of you as a child to be protected. As someone precious to me. Someone I couldn't bear to lose. But if I'm to love you truly, Surpanakha, I must protect you, yes, but I must first be *one* with you. I must learn to love what *you* love, to face what *you* fear and. . . " Harsha shook his head. "I thought of my sister, Chitra Gurung. I thought of what would happen if *she* were lost. If *she* were in the jungle—or if it were you or my brother Chiranjeev. Or, by Kaala, anyone I *loved*—and I were out here waiting. I'd go in without hesitation, *damn* the strictures of Chamundi's hunting grounds. If I'm to love you truly, Surpanakha—the real you, not some dainty, clay princess doll—then. . . " he shrugged, "this is the way."

Oh Shiva! Your fire. Your courage. You are the kindest, bravest, fiercest being that I've ever known. She felt her eyes moisten just a little. "But you still think it's risky?" she asked.

"What is love if it is never tested?" Harsha laughed, helping her stand. "One thing might help make it safer."

"What's that?"

"Next time you run into the jungle with your bow, perhaps take along some arrows." He pointed up to the level of the Sumukha Nivaasa, the Hall of Mirrors, to where her quiver lay forgotten. "Come on," he said, winking, "we've got a lot to do."

* * *

That night presented an opportunity for Surpanakha and Harsha's quest. The queen had dozed off in drunken languor, having consumed too much sura wine, face paint streaked from weeping and hair dishevelled from where she'd clawed at it in her grief. Kumbhakarna had locked himself inside the highest level of the Chandra Rajakula. He had sequestered in the Mukuta Mandir's training chamber, refusing to answer even to his sister. It had been days since he'd been seen. Harsha said he'd seen the prince on a balcony from the back of his pisacha.

Kumbhakarna was seen in a lotus posture with eyes shut tight, meditating. *Meditating. Kumbhakarna.* Never in all their years of martial training had her younger brother displayed such tenacity for the more. . . internal arts.

"Now that his older brother's gone," High Priest Shukra commented idly, "it seems Kumbhakarna's taken all of Ravan's energy into himself."

"Ravan's not gone," she responded. "And it's blasphemy for you to say so."

"What would you know of blasphemy, Princess?" the High Priest sneered. "You think it's a woman's work to hunt and wrestle like men. The queen and I would prefer to see you adopt a more pious, more modest mien."

At that moment, she wanted to shove Shukra's ceremonial sceptre of divine authority right up his pompous backside. Of course, she didn't say it aloud—not to the priest—but Harsha thought it was quite funny.

"Someone's in a better mood," he observed as they packed for their journey, rolling chapatis and dried jerky into a compact bundle before stuffing it inside his pack.

"We're going to see him," she exclaimed. "I can feel it. I. . . thank you, Harsha."

"Surpanakha, my priyatama." Harsha cupped one side of her face with a tender hand, brushing his thumb along her jawline with a sad and knowing smile. "Of course. Of course."

The night was moonless. A veil of clouds blanketed the sky, starlight bleeding through as a faint and ghostly whisper. They flew on his dragon to the highest tower of the palace, the stone floor littered with the supplies they'd gathered. A light rain fell outside, but it would not last until dawn.

The heavy teak door to the stairwell that led to the Mukuta Mandir, the Crown Temple, beneath them, was locked and barred; Surpanakha had ordered it so her brother could 'hold his vigil and pray to Lord Shiva in silence.'

No one knew Harsha was at the palace. If anyone found out—especially her mother—there'd be a heavy price to pay. Harsha could be banished from the Sapta Kula, the seven tribes of the Vidyadharas. She could be sequestered to her rooms and kept there until a *swayamwaraa,* where a courageous Asuran noble would win her hand in a competition of wits and valour.

Bloody beard of Shiva, she cursed. It could start a murderous war with the Vidyadharas if her family suspected anything. Courting the prince of another race was forbidden. Not officially. But the Devas mandated that all such relationships be brought to their attention. The hated occupiers would use any excuse, however trivial, to level accusations of treason.

As for Father. . . well. Pitr would be enraged if he found me consorting in private with the son of another kingdom. He'd probably say Harsha violated me. Just to start another bloody war. Or to protect my honour, of course.

"Surpanakha!" Harsha hissed, gesturing at the heavy wooden door. "Time presses! I'll finish up the packing."

"Right," she nodded, turning and hammering on the massive wooden door that led to the Crown Temple. "Kumbhakarna! Kumbhakarna! It's nearly time! If you want to join us, you need to do so now!"

Stillness, broken by intermittent flurries of rain. The whistling of the wind across the parapets.

"Kumbhakarna! Brother! Can you hear me?" she shouted. "Harsha! He can't hear me." She struggled at the latch on her side, but it was already open. Kumbhakarna had bolted the great teak door from the other side. "Bhratr, we must go to Ravan. We must help him."

"Surpanakha." Harsha glanced up from folding a sack containing a water masaka, buffalo jerky, herbs for healing, flint for fire, a copper pot for cooking, and a knife for cutting through the forest. The supplies would be essential to their survival. "If Kumbhakarna can't hear you, it's not due to the rain or wind." He tapped his head. And then, his heart.

"The rain and wind?" she snorted.

He grinned. "Kumbhakarna has heard you, trust me. He isn't coming with us."

"He's been in there for days! He needs to move. Hell, he needs to eat and drink. Does he really think that meditation will bring Ravan back?"

"Surpanakha." Harsha laced up his pack and hefted it, grinning as he settled it across his back. "We need to go. Now."

She tapped the great door thoughtfully, running through a list of mantras. *I could blast this thing open with a spell, storm in, and make my brother see sense. . .*

"You're right." She turned away. "He isn't coming."

"A pity." He helped her into her pack and then unrolled and showed her the map of the aranya on which they'd drawn their route. "We could have used his might and magic in the jungle."

Sweet, courageous Harsha, she thought with a smile. *My gentle flame.* Ravan understood her fire, and Kumbhakarna understood her fears. *But no one, indeed, feels my heart as Harsha does. He knows my tender, deep desires. My love of the ferocious jungle. My passion for healing children with raga-mantra magic, and of Ayurveda, the ancient science of healing.*

She smiled again, softly. No one knew her better than Harsha—for it was he who had stoked the flames of self-confidence and courage within her. It was he who had delved into the core of her being, peeled away the wall of so-called civilized behaviour in the palace, and shown her the precious heart of nature.

Perhaps—one day—they would be free to enjoy it. *But not today. Not as long as the Devas control Naraka.*

They descended the Chandra Rajakula, then went southwest, and climbed the Krodha Rajakula, a shorter spire that offered a view out across the tangled city roads beyond the palace walls.

The tangled city roads, then the plains, then the jungle.

She was breathless by the time she reached the top of Krodha Tower, though not for lack of strength. Whatever Father's objections about training 'the weaker sex' to fight, her uncle, Akampana, kept them in peak condition—Ravan and Kumbhakarna, her, and all their female cousins.

No. The reason Surpanakha's chest pumped like a bellows was the thought of what she and her love were about to do.

"Easy, Surpanakha," Harsha said, sliding his fingers up her neck. The base of her thick raven locks, stroking that tender skin at the back of her head, the place he knew she liked.

"You're not terrified?" she demanded, frowning as a sudden torrent of rain battered them at the top of the spire.

"Does fire burn in my belly?" Harsha asked, echoing her thoughts. "Does my heartbeat hammer in my chest? Of course, I'm scared, Surpanakha." He slid closer in the darkness, one hand on her neck and the other slipping her fingers into his own. "But who will comfort you if not me?"

She flushed. "You messed up my hair even worse than the rain had," she grumbled, bending away from Harsha's hand and readjusting the leather band that restrained her overabundance of hair. *Damn Mother and all her fashion stipulations. It would be far easier to hack the whole lot off.*

Uluka swooped down upon the southwest Rose Gate suddenly, emerging from a low-hanging cloud. He flapped his enormous wings with such rapidity that the torches on the battlement flickered suddenly beneath the gust.

She caught Harsha watching nervously, poised for the alarm to ring out.

Her eyes followed the flames from the torches, some of which had been snuffed out by the rain. The others shone like massive diyas in the night. She prayed that none of the guards had noticed. Alas, luck was not on her side. The scream of an Asuran guard pierced the silence of the night.

"Hey! Where do you think you're going?"

The guard was in the inner courtyard, near the southwest Rose Gate, not far from them. Surpanakha wasn't worried about being chased down; she mainly hoped that the guard would not alert the others. There'd be a great price to pay if they were caught. With a new rush of energy, Surpanakha tugged at her beloved's arm.

"Run!"

They ran nimbly along the parapets towards the southwest Rose Gate. As Surpanakha looked back, she noticed that the guard was alone. She squinted and then realized she *knew* him! With a short chuckle, Surpanakha smiled to herself. *Thank Shiva that the most incompetent of Father's guards chases after us.* Hemantha Kumaara wasn't prized for competence or speed. However, another guard now joined him. The two guards ran to the gate to reach Surpanakha and Harsha, hoping to prevent their escape by arresting them before they mounted Uluka.

Not a bad tactic, Surpanakha thought. *But it would need to be executed correctly. . .*

The gate was no cinch to climb. It was slippery due to fresh polish. The floral designs were too intricate to be a strong enough foothold. The second guard was fit, and he had no difficulty following Surpanakha and Harsha. His companion did not fare as well. Hemantha Kumaara tried to climb the gate and even succeeded in hoisting himself up, but the portly figure then lost his balance and dragged the other guard down with him. Surpanakha made a mental note to have Hemantha fired once she returned and to alert her father of the incompetents among his guards.

The two guards dusted themselves off and tried to climb the gate again. But by then, Surpanakha and Harsha had reached Uluka.

"Come, Uluka!" she said. "We're already away!"

"But what if they alert the others—" Harsha started.

"If they alert the others, we're already away," she laughed, scrambling up Uluka's scaly foreleg and leaping from the hollow of his shoulder back to the leather saddle Harsha had tailored especially for them. It allowed her to ride when she was wearing breeches and 'side-saddle' when she didn't have time to change out of the ridiculous saris that Mother made her wear.

Surpanakha readjusted herself on Uluka and marvelled at the pisacha's brilliance.

Vidyadharan dragons were terrifyingly possessive. Only a dragon's bonded rider could ever handle a grown pisacha's reins. They had to be trained for years to allow a howdah or a covered seat to be placed atop them and for a band of warriors to climb aboard them. The Vidyadharas sang many beautiful war ballads, but Surpanakha had always treasured the 'Legend of Krish-Tun Rai and Salaia Silverhair Gurung', a story of a vicious battle fought against Devan garuda eagles with hundreds of pisachas.

Harsha settled himself in before her, unfastening the reins and taking in their slack so he could guide Uluka as they flew up towards a tall spire with a cupola. After they had landed, safe from the guards or other prying eyes, Harsha bent down and fastened the straps about their legs with practised ease, allowing them just enough flexibility to move but not enough to fall off, should they be forced into any acrobatics.

"Just making sure we're secure," he told her with a grin. "As long as we're on Uluka, high in the clouds, we should be safe. When we land, that's when everything tries to kill us."

After long deliberation, they resolved to fly directly to the aranya before attempting to find Ravan's trail. Parts of the aranya were forbidden to Narakans and pisachas on pain of death. However, the routes that led to those regions were well known, and Surpanakha was confident they'd find her brother's tracks on one of the other main trails.

"Fly there first. Shukra used to take us hunting there," she told Harsha, pointing to a specific route. "Then circle along the perimeter. We'll touch down and investigate every trail until we find the one Ravan took."

From the landing point, they resolved to go on foot while the pisacha followed from above as best he could. Following the two of them from high above the jungle canopy would be arduous enough for Uluka. Trying to follow Ravan's twelve-day-old trail would be ten seasons past impossible from high in the sky. *Trying to track Ravan is like trying to track a damned shadow over the waters of the raging Sikatamayaa in monsoon season.*

"Right," her priyatama muttered, testing the straps and then shrugging his shoulders in preparation for the flight. "Rain in the eyes, no light to perceive by, and a brother's life to save. Any parting prayers to your Lord Shiva?"

"We've said our prayers," she muttered, glancing down across the palace complex architected by her father, with its beautiful Shiva temples, *rajakula* or palaces, rose gardens, and elevated pavilions with domed cupolas, a distinctive feature of Asuran architecture. A few scattered lamps winked amber from balconies. Bronze spearpoints glittered among the torches below them, and from the outer gates. A fountain in the centre of the inner courtyard babbled softly through the pattering of raindrops.

Other than that, Lanka, the immense capital of the Asuras, merely slumbered.

"Let's go." She wrapped her arms around Harsha's muscled core, pulled herself close, and bent her head as they were swept off into the rain.

Chapter 9

Twice-Born

Day Twelve

I will return today! Ravan felt the fire of *rajas* surging through his veins.

"Today, Sharabha," he murmured, tickling the creature beneath the chin. "Today, we are born again as *dvijas.* Or simurghs if you like. Fully dvija simurghs. Bah!"

He chuckled as Sharabha purred affectionately, snapping at his fingers. He felt the baby simurgh's tail coil behind him and lash his ribs. "Aah!" he mouthed.

After their third day together, the baby had refused the pack's shelter on Ravan's back. Most of the time, it crouched atop it, like one of the sculptures that flanked his father's throne.

The vultures bloodied you before I found you. A few deep scratches marred its downy stomach. *You lost blood from a deep peck to the throat. I'm surprised that you're recovering so fast.*

The simurgh had the unsettling habit of peering deep into his eyes for several minutes before looking away abruptly, jumping down from his perch and padding off into the brush to forage. He was surprised by its intelligence, as it seemed to mirror his moves and even pre-empt them sometimes.

How fast do your kind grow? Will you develop faster if trained? He began to feel a little intimidated.

As he prayed to Pashupati, lord of the animals, that he wasn't bringing home a disaster, the twice-topped hill named Dvi Parvata came into view.

"We're almost home!" the prince cried, skipping ahead. *I know this place intimately.* He was outside the aranya now, nearing the haunts of his childhood.

"Today, we're twice-born. Dvijas!" he exclaimed as Sharabha leaped down from his pack, landing on a boulder beside him and darting off, tail flicking. "Don't go far," he called out, to no avail, then settled back with a chuckle against the boulder. It was smooth and warmed by several hours of sunshine.

By Murugan's vel, he breathed, *I need to rest.* His back throbbed to the eternal beat of the Onam River festival's drums. The pain joined the dull ache of hunger that pounded at his temples. Now and then, it lanced with sudden fury when he stumbled over the ever-present dipterocarp roots and cracked his wounds open.

As he rested on the boulder, however, his body started going numb.

Numbness. That's bad.

Bad, bad, bad, he thought, watching the bounce in Sharabha's tail as the rascally creature went darting off among the rocks. *One of us is getting better. The other nears death.*

"We'll make it back today," he groaned, "barely." Both the Teacher and Shukra had taught him to push himself to his limits and then go beyond. He'd been wounded before, gone without food, even used magic to defeat poison. *I've stumbled feverishly through other patches of the aranya and survived.*

Every time he prevailed, learned something of immense value. *It all adds up to this moment,* he thought, through the numbness that slowly enveloped his mind. Ravan found his mind drifting in a hell he didn't know existed. *I've never been this close to entering Kaala's halls.*

"We'll make it!" he hissed, battling to stand up. *Not here. I can't rest here.* "We will make it. Sharabha!" He staggered up and stumbled across the boulders, scanning for the creature's tail. "Sharabha! We're going." *Where is that creature? Why is it always running—*

Something flashed across the rock to his left, a blur of shadowy flesh and muscle just outside his vision.

He spun and tried to roar, to emit a sound designed to give any wild creature pause. Instead, what emerged was a low moan suspended by a single string, swaying in a gale of terror and vulnerability.

"Sharabha!" He collapsed with a gasp as the little one bounded towards him. *Damned simurgh. Damned Trial.*

"I can't even see straight, Sharabha," he whispered. "We need to get back soon. No way in Kaala's halls am I leaving you here al—"

His words trailed off, panic spiking through his gut.

Sharabha was frozen in a crouch. The creature's tail hooked stiffly, ears raised in alarm.

"Sharabha?" Ravan whispered. The throbbing of his back and the numbness of his legs faded for a moment, lending him the clarity needed to snatch up his khukris and peer in the direction the simurgh had locked on to. Sensing the air, listening to the wind. "Sharabha?"

The simurgh only hunched lower, the slightest of growls rippling from its throat as it stared towards. . . *nothing.* Then, Sharabha turned towards Ravan and darted over between his feet with a warning growl.

"Sharabha?" Ravan edged backward, reaching slowly for his bow. *How far? Do I have time to nock an arrow?* Sharabha peered into some bushes, unmistakably focused on something. *Surely nothing can cover the ground in. . .*

His fingers closed on the dhanush, and as he drew it forward, his other hand scrambled for the quiver that lay alongside his pack. His hand brushed against some fletching; he reached back and pulled the arrow out smoothly, letting the entire quiver slide down the rock towards him with the motion. It bumped to a halt against his leg, feathers tickling his calf.

What is it, boy? He slid the arrow forward over the bow and slid its nock across the string. *Ready.*

"Boy?" he whispered, his voice anxious as he felt Sharabha trembling under him. The simurgh stood frozen, ears pointed, shoulders knotted beneath those tawny feathers.

Slowly Ravan stilled, sinking his *aatma,* his consciousness, into the area around him. Into the tiny little fleck of the realm, the sliver in which he and Sharabha were ensconced.

The part that was trying to kill him.

ॐ भूर्भुवः स्वः ।
तत्सवी- तुवरण्यम ।

(O Supreme Being, Embodiment of vital energy, Bestower of happiness.)

He whispered the mantra, breathing himself throughout the soul of the place. The life that curled through the ferns that blanketed the red earth. The stirring of the shaala leaves in the breeze. The basking of death mask orchids in the bushes around them.

Nothing. I feel nothing. The ground swam beneath Ravan's feet, and spots danced in front of his eyes. His strength drained faster than the purse of a pious farmer to priests at the Asuran temples in Ucchitapura.

ॐ तत्पुरुषाय विद्महे महादेवाय धीमहितन्नो रुद्रः प्रचोदयात ।

> (Om. Let me meditate on the great Purusha, Oh, Lord Shiva, give me higher intellect and let the great God Rudra illuminate my mind.)

And the wind stirred. And stilled. And spooled away into nothing. Sharabha spat in alarm and twisted, clearly unnerved by the spell. Ravan listened. *Nothing.* Their potential enemy—whatever it was—had not caught their scent since it was upwind of them.

Softly, he eased his magical control over the area, allowing the breeze to build back up. By the time it did, Sharabha had darted forward, crouching alongside a boulder, and peered down into the bushes yet again.

Impossible to see, Ravan muttered silently, reaching out with his mind. *Nothing. Third eye of Shiva, there's nothing there!*

Coincidence, that whatever it was had happened along at just the right moment to startle little Sharabha.

But the creature's senses were sharper than his; he was sure of that. *Trust the essence of the wild,* the Teacher whispered. *A trained Asuran mind cannot be beaten on Naraka. Likewise, Asuran eyes aided by magic cannot be defeated, except by the very best of raptors.*

"Let the wild ones be your ears, your nose," Ravan whispered, studying the land around him. His grasp on his dhanush weakened, and his senses waxed dull. *I should be keenly attuned to the plants, creatures, even insects around me. Especially the insects. . .*

After what seemed an eternity, birds began to sing. Nature's sounds returned in a trickle, then a flood. Sharabha relaxed and sat fully upright, ears twitching at the sudden deluge of sound. *He seems calmer now—a good sign.*

Unless our hunter is more cunning than most or has magic, Ravan thought uneasily, shouldering his pack and motioning to the baby simurgh. "Come on," he muttered. "We're leaving."

We're safe for the moment.

* * *

When the Mahadev Yaagamandapa Temple appeared hours later, Ravan heaved a great sigh. For nearly a full minute, he stood there, rubbing at his eyes, expecting at any minute for the massive temple complex to dissolve into nothingness. But the great shrine of his forefathers glowed in the distance, lit by a thousand diyas of light.

"We made it, Sharabha," he whispered hoarsely, collapsing on the grass, tears forming in his eyes. His hands trembled as he brushed the verdant grass, looking back in awe at the aranya. Many moons prior, Vaasuki had laughed and said the Trial was but a symbol, a long-dried husk of meaningless ritual.

"She was wrong," Ravan said with conviction, forcing himself to his feet and drying his tears. The wounds on his shoulder had begun to open; pain radiated down his spine with increasing vigour. Then, with a short mantra, he scattered its intensity, embracing the numbness one last time. *I'm not finished,* he thought. *Blood of Shiva, she was wrong. I almost died through the challenge.*

Something isn't right. Ravan arrived at the massive wood and metal of the Hemapushpa Raajadvaara, the Rose Gate, which guarded the southwest city wall. He'd expected to be greeted by his entire family, by large numbers of nobles and citizens, cheering and praising the great God Mahadeva for bringing their yuvaraaja back to them. *All of Lanka knows I was away on the Trial of Seven Days. It isn't every day that your firstborn prince sets off to die a boy. To be reforged in Aran Yani's fire. Perfected in the harsh smithy of the Jungle Goddess.*

The people of Asurapura love me. Father prefers warring and whoring to watching over his people. But in the king's absence, Ravan had visited every part of the Asuran Empire. He had sat with Asurans young and old, rich and poor, priests and laypeople alike. He listened to their appeals, recording their challenges, hopes, and dreams, dispensing justice, helping as well as he could.

In the weeks before his Trial, mountains of letter scrolls, *prashaad,* rudrakshas, and amulets had arrived, sent by his people from all over Asurapura. He couldn't possibly have carried them all with him.

But he'd taken one for memory. To honour their piety and love. *They are my people, and they love me dearly.*

Then why are they so quiet now?

Ravan approached the Rose Gate with the last ounce of strength he could muster. He was weak, but he wouldn't show it. The structure was unsullied, with no signs of the paint chipping. The rustic hue shone in brilliance; gazing upon it, Ravan felt proud to be an Asuran. Adorned with gems in the Vidyadharan Rai technique, with finely cut precious stones from various parts of the kingdom. Turquoise from Ratnapur juxtaposed sharply with the pastoral architecture and radiated with brilliance. Jade peeked out from between the turquoise and complemented the other colours. *What Vishravasura pitr lacks in the ability to govern, he compensates for with his passion for architecture and the grand structures he commissions throughout the Asuran kingdom.*

And then, his expression soured. *Wonder how many slaves died under the Devan whip securing these gems,* Ravan thought bitterly.

It began subtly, with the guard who hailed him from the battlements. "My Prince! You've made it! By the Destroyer, my Prince! We thought you were lost."

"So did I." Ravan grinned weakly, sagging against his bow and struggling to hide the pain. *The people need me to burn brightly, a brand of hope against the terrors of the realm.* Those words of the ancient Asuran emperor, Kubera, applied now more than ever, with Naraka suffering under the lash of Chakravarthi Indra.

"So did I, my soldier. Now get these gates open and let your twice-born prince into his city to see his people!" *A twice-born. I am dvija at last.*

The barest hint of a smile appeared on Ravan's face as the massive thirty-foot metal and wood gates swung open. He hobbled forward to enter his great city.

It was then that he noticed the guard hadn't given much more than a quick, superficial response. That the sentry was alone. That he hadn't even mentioned the simurgh, whose head poked up from Ravan's backpack.

"There should be more of you, my man," he observed lightly as the sentry came trotting down the inner battlement.

"Right, my Prince!" The man saluted and hastened forward, offering a water masaka and reaching for Ravan's bow. "You see, there's—"

"I will keep my things," Ravan answered calmly, leaning on his bow. "And I will not drink until I've looked upon the queen's face. I will bear my burden until I reach the palace steps, as is the tradition."

He then muttered "Peace!" to Sharabha, who had begun to stir. *It won't be easy carting a simurgh through the chaos of central Lanka. Perhaps I should have entered through the secret tunnels that lead right into the palace.*

No. Let my people see that their prince is back. Let them see that I'm twice-born.

As for this guard. . . "And my question?" he pressed. "Where are your comrades, soldier?"

The guard swallowed. "My Prince. The men are here, in the city."

"Hardly reassuring. Where else would they go?"

"They uh. . . well, my Prince, they are with the Vidyadharans."

"The Vidyadharas?" *What are the Vidyadharas doing here? Has Harsha announced his desire to court Surpanakha?* If so, it was far too early in their relationship. *Father will have Harsha horsewhipped and cast out of the kingdom.*

"My Prince. The Vidyadharas have come to discuss the disappearance of their crown prince, Harsha Gurung." The soldier's voice was strained. *He's hiding something disastrous.*

"Soldier!" Ravan barked, wincing as he felt the pain flare. "You will tell me every single thing of import that is going on here. Slowly and clearly."

"Yes, my Prince," he quavered, glancing about. "You see, it's your sister and Harsha. They've—"

"My Prince! Yuvaraaja Ravan." Someone came galloping down the central road, waving excitedly as he approached.

"Commander Prahasta," Ravan greeted the tall Asuran on his stout pony, heart quaking when he saw the commander's anxiety. "Tell me what in all of Kaala's hells is going on." *Has Surpanakha run off with the Vidyadharan prince? Has she announced their love to the public?*

"Your sister and Prince Harsha," Prahasta gasped, reining his horse to a halt. "They've vanished. We think they went into the aranya."

A great, rolling laugh emerged from Ravan's lips.

"My Prince?" Prahasta said, his face contorted with worry. Ravan didn't answer the Asuran commander. He clutched at his bow like a drowning Rakshasa grasping at the keel of a *porkkappal,* a battleship, and doubled over, his body racked by shrill laughter.

This is just so funny. Don't they see?

"I passed through hell!" he shrieked. "I died and rose again! I was hunted by Devas. I faced a mother simurgh and triumphed!" *I walked for days with the lifeblood draining out of my body, every step a numbing torment.* "And I've come back to learn that. . . " he howled, hanging on to his bow and swaying as he looked Prahasta in the eye. *My sweet, sweet anujaa is missing. My baby sister. How will Mother survive the shock?*

"You. . . you will find them!" Ravan blabbered, blinking dazedly, a wave of panic enveloping his mind, drowning out all thought. Then, there was a great noise, a roar in his ears. "You. . . curse you all! How could you let this happen?!"

Then his fingers slipped, and he lurched sideways, the pack pulling him down, as Sharabha jumped out into Prahasta's arms. He felt himself falling. Spinning.

Darkness. . .

Chapter 10

The Spinning of a Blossom as it Falls

Day Twelve

Surpanakha couldn't get the image out of her mind. Ravan's lifeless body on the jungle floor. Harsha and she had reached the aranya's borders without incident and dismounted from the Vidyadharan prince's pisacha, Uluka. The great dragon now flew overhead as they approached the thicket.

Progress was difficult. They found footsteps on two of the narrow paths leading in,, and Harsha chose what was, in Surpanakha's opinion, clearly the wrong route.

Uluka was attacked in the air while they explored the jungle floor. A simurgh came screeching out of trees miles distant—a massive, hook-winged shape with a roar that made the forest go silent. The monster zeroed in on Uluka's position above the canopy with breathtaking accuracy.

Surpanakha and Harsha could only watch flickers of the battle through the thick canopy as the Vidyadharan's bond mate fought for its life. Uluka was massive, far bigger than the average simurgh, and enjoyed a thick hide with interlocking scales. Still, the ancient tales described simurghs as fierce, sharp-clawed, and incredibly territorial.

"My Uluka will dispatch him in no time with salt bombs from his glands," remarked Harsha. After the fight, Uluka joined them on the jungle floor so Surpanakha could heal and bind some of his deep wounds. "You're such a natural *vaidya* with your Asuran mantras and herbs," remarked Harsha.

"These wounds won't kill Uluka, but they'll slow him down and take an age to heal if they aren't attended to right away," Surpanakha said grimly. She gently chanted a healing mantra while binding a laceration on the pisacha's left wing with linen from her love's pack.

After that, Uluka simply turned, flew up, and took off in the direction of the Great Peaks. He flew towards the land of the Vidyadharas in the northeast, resentfully following Harsha's hummed instructions to leave him and Surpanakha behind and fly home. Vidhyadharan songs were powerful, allowing communication with dragons and even other beasts.

* * *

"And that's why I think we should have taken the other route," Surpanakha griped.

"Priyatama. My love. There are probably several simurghs in this jungle, and they'll attack any pisacha that intrudes on their territory. So, I hardly expect the other route would have been safer."

"I just don't get it," she sighed. "The other route had a single chain of marks, ones so subtle that no one but Ravan would leave them."

Harsha groaned and rubbed his temple, peering into the dense foliage. "We've been through this, Surpanakha. The other route had many tracks, true. But think! Ravan's been gone far too long. We're here because we think he ran into trouble. It's possible that someone or something is hunting him, and he's evading them. Or he's tracking something. He could have run into wilder Nagas on the way. Each of those is a good reason for his delay. If the marks you mention were his alone, there's no great need for worry."

Surpanakha sighed and followed him. Still, a shiver ran down her spine. *Trouble. Someone or something. Hunted. Dark possibilities. Damn this Trial to Shiva's third eye.*

"I know," she grunted. "I know. It's just that I don't want to believe he ran into. . . " She cursed. "We saw at least eight sets of tracks on the trail, Harsha. Ten, if you count those hoofprints of Kinnaras." But Harsha refused to believe that the denizens of the great Narakan desert and the steppe to the far northwest had galloped hundreds of miles to the aranya.

My love is a good tracker, she reassured herself. Vidyadharan trackers predicted *patterns* of movement through terrain rather than following *specific* spoor or signs. Surpanakha found it akin to witchcraft, but Harsha claimed it had to do with 'understanding Shakti's nature and hearing Her Song.' *What does that even mean?* the Asuran princess thought. Whatever it was, he followed the sparse trail with an eerie accuracy.

Ahead, her priyatama cursed and leaped aside as something scuttled across the path. "It's a giant beetle, love," she observed drily, restraining a giggle as his hand went to his deadly curved knife. The Vidyadharan *bichuwa* was especially lethal at close quarters.

"Stupid *bhrga!*" Harsha cursed, slamming his blade back into its sheath. "It skittered across my foot!"

"Perhaps you were in its way," she chuckled. "Speaking of which, do you mind if we contin—"

There was a brief rustling in the undergrowth, and then something snapped against her right foot, caught her ankle, and sent her sprawling. It had moved swiftly beneath the soil.

A net, she realized in horror. A few feet ahead, Harsha was flung headlong with a cry, then jerked up into the air.

Frantically, she clawed at the ground with her hands, but thick fibres of netting caught her fingers and bent them as a hefty hemp rope pulled her sharply into the air.

For a moment, she spun about, and the forest echoed with her curses. "Quiet! Scimitar of Kali, be quiet!" Harsha hissed. He scrambled for his knife. "Cut your way out bef—"

Then they heard the laughter.

All things crafted by those around them, she thought. *A flame in the wind, a voice in the darkness, the spinning of a hibiscus blossom. . . as it falls.*

Chapter 11

Living with Lies

Day Thirteen

Ravan awoke to familiar smells. His face was pressed into the soft pillow of his bed. He twisted to see the beautiful bronze oil lamps that hung from the ceiling right above him. He squinted, and tiny lights danced on the ceiling. To his right was the exquisite *darpana,* or mirror, that captured the imagination. Adorned with yellow sapphires and rubies from the great mines of Naraka, they shone with a shy brilliance as the light from the diyas hit the gems.

As a child, he'd peer at the rubies and see flames dancing within them. The walls and floors of the Shri Nivaasa, the yuvaraja's apartments, were white marble that had a cooling effect in the blazing summers. Vidyadharan artisans had laboured in the familiar *parchin kari* style for many months to create stunning images on the walls of the sprawling quarters. The inlay technique of using cut and fitted, highly polished coloured stones, such as rubies, yellow sapphires, and topaz, had been honed to perfection by the Vidyadharas in the Peaks over millennia. *I don't even like those gems. They make the room look tawdry.* Then, Ravan saw his reflection in the darpana. *I look like a furball coughed up by a simurgh!*

Slowly, he regained his senses. Gates of memory opened, and memories of the Trial flooded his mind in shocking detail. He felt a strange coolness at the nape of his neck. It spread deliciously across his upper back. Someone was working away at his wounds, applying a soothing balm.

Wounds? He struggled upwards with a groan, twisting to see where—

"Sit. Sit! Please!" Someone pushed him gently but firmly down to the bed.

Begrudgingly, he twisted his head sideways, allowing himself a partial view of the room. His mind spun. *Wounds. . . bed. . . hands. Marvellous job, Ravan.*

"What's going on?" he grunted. "What am I. . .? "

Surpanakha. He stiffened. "Surpanakha!" It came in a visceral rush. The fear. The uphill battle for survival. The triumph of coming home a dvija.

Then, horror, panic, anger. And finally, guilt.

"Surpanakha!" With a snarl, he twisted himself free of the hands that urged him to stay down, thrust himself to one side of the bed, and spun, looking for his bow. "Where is she? Why did you let me sleep, by Kaala's dark halls!" A pair of ornate ceremonial gold spears flanked the mantle. His bow was nowhere to be seen.

"Bring me Commander Vriko Dhara!" Ravan shouted, kicking himself free of the blankets and trying to leap out of the bed. He would've landed face first on the cool, hard marble if a pair of strong hands hadn't caught him about the waist. The wounds along his back cracked, and a trickle of hot blood emerged. In a trice, he was back on his stomach on the bed.

Grimly, his captors tied the prince's wrists to the bedposts, ignoring his threats and vain attempts to escape.

"You have not healed, my Prince!" someone spoke up in a deep voice. "Do you remember, Yuvaraja Ravan? Do you remember what happened in the Trial?"

"I remember," the prince growled. "I remember everything." *EVERYTHING! Surpanakha is gone. My little sister's gone, and everyone's just sitting here.* "Why aren't you searching for my *anujaa*?"

"You're hurting. I understand," High Priest Shukra remarked in a grave tone.

By Kaala, Lord of the Black Halls, how many are in my quarters? Mother and her entourage, Shukra and his. Kumbhakarna and his. Laboriously, Ravan turned his head to the other side of the bed, knowing what he'd find.

My guards, huddled together, faces pinched with worry. Good old Maho-Dhara, first of my hunters. The stout Asura stood closest to the headboard. His hands wrung anxiously together, coated in fresh blood.

"Why are your hands trembling? Why are they bleeding?"

"Er. . . this is *your* blood, my Prince," Maho-Dhara said. "You slipped from the bed. I had to catch you."

"Oh. Of course." *I tried to get up, tried to. . .*

"Why'd you try to get up, foolish boy?" his mother snipped, applying something over his back once more. *Incredible. Refreshing. Seems to drink the pain away.*

"Completely trashed my job of this garlic, cloves, and arnica ointment," his mother continued. "It's a wonder the stitches didn't burst, the way y—"

"I asked you a question," Ravan growled. He hated speaking into the pillow, like an old man too weak to even lift himself out of bed.

"Why is Kumbhakarna standing here instead of leading a search party into the aranya?"

"We are scouring our lands, my son. Asuran scouts and warriors are out right now, as many as we can spare. You think I'd risk your brother's life in the jungle?"

You let my sister leave, he thought bitterly. "Bring me my bow and khukris. Extra bandages, needle and thread, and a full pack."

"You are not leaving this chamber." His mother's voice was sharp as a straight razor and brittle as thin ice. "You'll hardly make it out of the city before you collapse."

"Your mother is right," Shukra intoned gravely. "You cannot leave these chambers until we have pronounced you healed, and—"

"My sister is in the jungle!" Ravan hissed. "Do you think I'd rest here while—"

"You are in no shape to go." *Kumbhakarna's voice, stony as ever but tinged with compassion. He feels my pain. Why does he not go after them?*

After a long moment of tension, Ravan sighed. "Very well, Matr. I'm in no shape to go. You're right." *Kumbhakarna is the steady one, the rock who loomed from a sea of chaos.*

"I trust Kumbhakarna," he muttered thickly, and now in blind anger, "not you, Shukra."

"Even as you say, my Prince." The high priest bowed his head.

"You should address the high priest of all Asurapura with more respect!" His mother's voice was icy. "Forgive him, High Priest Shukra."

"No forgiveness needed." There was a rustle of silk as the old man bowed smoothly. "He's suffering, his mind confused."

Ravan laughed. "What confuses me is this—how could my sister have slipped out without a soul knowing?" A thousand plans whirled through his mind, all of them rash and ill-considered. "Shukra." His voice was a hideous croak.

"My Prince?"

He tried to sound as forceful as possible.

"Did you pronounce me twice-born? Dvija?"

"My Prince." The high priest's voice was uncertain. "You passed the Trial. Of that there can be no doubt. However, your return was quite delayed and somewhat. . . unexpected."

"I fully expected him to succeed," Kumbhakarna interjected gravely. His hands were folded with typical sobriety. "I never doubted for a moment, brother."

"*Anujaa,* I don't think I greeted you." He was glad to see Kumbhakarna. *"Still...* Why are you not searching for our dear anujaa?"

Kumbhakarna didn't flinch. He'd expected his brother's reproach; it didn't faze him.

"This isn't a goats and tigers game, people!" Ravan screeched. "This is my little sister! So go out there and find them!"

"Son!" Kaikesi's hands stopped their soothing motion. "If you weren't injured, I'd have you punished for such talk."

Ravan battled back a laugh.

Shukra frowned. "You are laughing. Why?"

"It's just so funny. Don't you think it's funny?" Ravan appealed to Kumbhakarna. "They threaten us with punishment as if it's *us* that suffer! The Devas threaten us, the noble houses. But it's not *us* they take as slaves." *We live in luxury, and our people bear the whip. And the taxes.*

Abruptly, the room went silent.

"Ravan?" His mother sounded frightened. "Be quiet for a moment." There was a flurry of movement in the room as the personal guard, retinues, and servants filed out. In moments, only his mother, Shukra and Kumbhakarna remained.

"What did you say, Prince?" Shukra knelt to peer into Ravan's eyes.

He ignored the man. The high priest's face grew darker. "Did you not hear my question?"

"I'm ignoring you, *gurudev*. Mother?"

"Ravan." His mother's voice was tinged with worry. "Are you dizzy? Do you see spots? How much do you remember, of wha—"

"I'm lucid, my dear matr," he sighed. *Perhaps I'm being too harsh.* "Sorry. Forgive me. It's just. . . " He held back a giggle. "So long! For centuries, we nobles have lived like snivelling cowards, frightened of the Devan whip."

"My son," Kaikesi began tenuously, "you've been through a lot, and—"

"My sister is lost," he grumbled, "and you speak of what *I've* been through? I nearly died in the aranya, Mother! For years, you indulged me in this palace. Not to say I didn't train in the Ring of Trying. Didn't suffer in the aranya under High Priest Shukra's watchful eye... " Ravan laughed bitterly.

"Yuvaraja." Shukra placed his hand on the prince's head. "What did you say about the Devas?"

"The Devas?" *So humiliating, the years of bowing and scraping in front of the Devas.* "They enslave our people! We sit around and eat mangoes and allow them to—"

"Blood of Shiva, boy, be quiet!" his mother hissed, slapping him across the face. And then, she took a step back, her face turning pale. "Sorry. I'm sorry, my son. You're weak. It's just. . . by Kaala, Ravan! We don't know if there's a Devan spy among us! Saraswathi Nandan keeps a close eye on us all. These are treasonous words you speak, and. . . "

Saraswathi Nandan, that pompous Devan overseer of Lanka. But as Ravan listened to his mother rattle on, he realized he'd been rash.

I have to live with the lies until I'm strong enough to challenge the power that looms over us. The power of Chakravarthi Indra.

By the time his mother had finished, he was in check, nodding and muttering apologies like a powerful but docile water buffalo at an Asuran farm. *I will bide my time.*

His family and Shukra left his chambers seemingly mollified, and he found himself alone once more. Only one thing pressed on his mind.

Surpanakha is still missing.

Chapter 12

Ripples

Ravan's convalescence was tortuously slow. The vaidyas came every day for the first four days, walking through the heavily guarded Leheriya Rajadvaara gates, climbing the stairs to the sixth level of the Chandra Rajakula Palace, and into his apartments in the Shri Nivaasa. The physicians were headed by his tigress of a mother. Every day, they checked his bandages and fed him vermicelli *payasa* cooked in sweetened milk, as well as goat meat, and *poorana,* sweet flatbread. He ate laboriously—bite by tiny bite—as they urged him to sip a noxious herbal concoction with his head propped up like a hen at the cutting block. They changed his linen bandages every second day, cleaned the green-grey pus on his infected lacerations, and rubbed his back with ointments of garlic paste, turmeric, coconut oil, and tea tree oil.

The vaidyas instructed him to move as little as possible. But of course, as soon as they left, he struggled from the softness of his bed and lurched about his sprawling quarters. He was shocked by the frailty of his own flesh.

"Maho-Dhara, First of my Hunters!" Ravan called out from his door down a long corridor. Moments later, the powerful young Asura appeared and bowed.

"My Prince."

"How is Sharabha? Are his wounds being treated? What are they feeding my boy?"

"Yuvaraaja, the baby simurgh now lives at the quarters of your esteemed uncle, Arch Blade Ranger Akampana. Your uncle feeds Sharabha a special diet and has even begun its training. The baby grows faster than any being in the known realms and seems extremely intelligent for a beast."

"Hmmm," sighed the prince. "I had grown quite close to the rascal. As soon as I'm healed, I will take over his training myself. But for now, he is in good hands. Go, Maho-Dhara. Get some rest."

As the fifth day neared, he was sure that he would snap. "I conquered the aranya, and here I am, struggling to walk," he hissed in disgust, hobbling from ornate bedpost to bedpost and then along the pristine marble walls covered with colourful paintings of the various forms of Shiva. It was dark, and the palace, except for the royal guard, was asleep. The pain grew as light dimmed over the kingdom. As the Sun Elemental Surya descended into the western horizon, fair-haired demons crept from the shadows of his mind and leaped, fully incarnate, about the room. Shrieking simurghs and red-eyed hounds and Devan halberdiers with hands bloodied to the elbow.

With my sister's blood, he thought. But he never saw her in his nightmares. Only her screams, piercing the bones of his inner ear. *Only her plaintive cries.*

Nights were when he most needed a distraction, so he forced himself up and paced the room in agony, a wounded beast circling its cage. *Soon,* he swore. *Soon I will be strong enough. I'll slip out in the dead of night find my sister and Harsha. And bring them home.*

Ravan grimaced as he turned a corner in the room, ribs protesting. "I marched with two dead vultures in my pack and a bloody simurgh on my shoulders. So why am I weaker now than I was in the middle of that hell?"

"It's only natural," a deep voice suddenly spoke up, "injured as you are."

"Spear of Muruga!" he swore, diving to the bedstand, fumbling for his trusty khukris. He muttered a spell of protection. . .

ॐ त्र्यम्बकं यजामहे सुगन्धिं पुष्टिवर्धनम्. . .

(Om, we worship the three-eyed One, who is fragrant as the spiritual essence, increasing the nourishment of our spiritual core.. .)

Abruptly, Ravan stopped, realizing who had spoken. "Teacher!"

"Forgot my voice already? What Asurapura is gossiping about must be true. You really are going mad." There was a quiet chuckle, and then, the shadows in a corner of Ravan's chambers shifted. The darkness rippled for a moment. Then a man stepped forward, taking shape from nothing.

"You. . . how did you do that?" Flushing, Ravan rammed his khukris back into their sheaths and collapsed, trembling on his bed. *Shiva's blood.* "You scared me, Teacher! What in all of Kaala's halls are you trying to prove by sneaking into the palace?"

"I thought it might be time for me to pay you a visit. That I would like to see my star pupil, my *shikshak,*" the Teacher responded airily, "and confirm the rumours for myself."

He approached Ravan, eyes darting all over his pupil's body. "I see that they are, as all rumours, a mix of truth and fiction."

"I'm not half-mad, if that's what you're implying," Ravan grumbled. "I should have expected a visit from you, Teacher."

"Yes," the old man nodded. "You should have. But it was rather amusing, seeing you hop like a first-year Lankan infantry cadet reaching for his toad-sticker khanda."

"I didn't expect you in the middle of the night. Certainly not leaping from the shadows like a demon from the Shiva Purana, the chronicles of The Destroyer. How in the fourth hall of Kaala did you do that, and why haven't you taught me the spell?"

"You haven't been paying attention," the man admonished, settling himself at the foot of the bed, folding his powerful hands before him. The Teacher was a distinctly older man—grey beard, grey hair, wrinkles across the face and eyes.

Ravan had no idea how old the man might be. *Seventy? Sixty? A weather-beaten fifty? Or far, far older, perhaps?* Sometimes, the man spoke of thousand-year-old historical events as if he'd witnessed them first-hand. At other times, he made absurd statements such as 'if I ever reach adulthood,' sounding like a child.

He was a Teacher like no other, his lessons simple one day and maddeningly complex the next. He was the greatest mystery in Ravan's life but also a profound anchor. *The anchor that my father should've been.*

The only questions the man did not allow were questions about himself.

The wise sage was dressed as always in a simple homespun eight-yard cotton *pancha kachcham* or five-fold dhoti. The pancha kachcham was worn to facilitate fast movement, especially when fighting. The Teacher was the most terrifying opponent Ravan had ever faced, whether with sword or spell. Tall and broad-chested, with the muscles of his stomach hard and flat.

"*I* haven't been paying close attention?" Ravan gestured towards the shadows at the door to the *avaskara,* or privy." *Were the shadows darker before?* "The privy leads to nowhere. I didn't see anyone enter my door. A moment ago, I was alone, and the next, you leaped out from the darkness. Are you saying travelling through space is a trick you have taught me? Because, if so, I've forgotten."

"There's no such thing as a 'trick,'" the Teacher grunted, clapping his hands twice together. Flame magically leaped onto every lamp in Ravan's room. "I've told you that."

"Yes," Ravan muttered dryly. "You also told me you avoided Lanka."

"You've skipped too many lessons already. By not coming to see me, you've forced me to come to you."

"Skipped?" Ravan laughed. "Not coming? I had the bloody Trial to face, Teacher! You knew that."

"The Trial ended days ago," his master replied mildly. "And don't say bloody. It ill becomes a boy, much less a prince."

"A boy no longer," Ravan corrected. "I'm twice-born now, Teacher. With your training and blessings, I succeeded."

"Did you now?" A smile touched the corners of the old man's lips.

Infuriating, the way he smiles.

"Tell me what you've learned."

"I tracked Devas," the prince listed them. "I lost their hounds with magic, I fought a simurgh, I rescued its baby from the—"

"But what have you *learned,* Ravan? What gives you such certainty to stand and say 'I am twice-born?'"

Blood of Kaala. I hoped something might be different now that I have passed the Trial.

"You say leadership is a journey." He sighed wearily. "You're right. But. . . Shiva's blood, I've learned a great deal! I've learned the Devas whip us. They cage us like animals in the mines. I've learned Asuras give aid to Rakshasas in the jungle, and Nagas use their thermal vision to serve as Devan sentries."

"You came back with many more questions than answers," the Teacher murmured, blue eyes burning as they pierced his soul.

"I. . . yes." Ravan nodded simply. "That's as good a summary as any."

"So. Tell me of your ripples."

Ravan sighed. This was the customary exercise at the beginning of their lessons. Ravan was to be still as a pond. The wind was above, the stones beneath, and a hundred animals sipped at his waters. Worries, nipping at his mind. The material dimension, demanding his attention. One by one, he'd turn to analyze the things that tugged at him, and one by one, he would smooth them over. He would seek to be glass-smooth, as still as the heart of midnight, a mere reflection of the world around him.

"Surpanakha is missing," he burst out helplessly, stomach clenching as he said the words. "And I've been stuck here for days!"

"I heard." The Teacher nodded gravely. "What word?"

"None. Our warriors found several trails, and they're following every single one. But the Asuran infantry are like Devan elephants trampling a flower garden. They're useless in the dense aranya."

"They're not that bad." The Teacher frowned. "Asuras and Nagas are native to this realm. They know it as well as any."

He sighed. "I suppose you're right. But it's been centuries since we even considered the aranya ours! The Devas forbid us to enter its inner circle, and its mythical beasts fill our legends with horror. Three Asuran search parties have been attacked by bands of wilder Nagan archers. Five others got lost, wandering for days before they were found again. Commander Vrikodhara claims they were led astray by false trails."

"And the Vidyadharas?"

"Nearly as bad." He shook his head. "They continue to search, but they can't see anything from the air, and simurghs harry their pisacha dragons. Harsha's pisacha is nowhere to be seen. Anyway, I think the Devas have somehow warded off the interior aranya with their magic."

"Very perceptive, Ravan. And you?" The Teacher studied Ravan intensely. "What lies in your power to do?"

"Sit here for now," he sighed. *I know where this is going.* "But, Teacher, it's not working this time. I can't be a calm pond under these circumstances."

"Why ever not?" The old man looked surprised.

"Because it's never been like this before!" *I hate it when the Teacher plays games.* "It's never been someone this close to me."

"What did you think we were training for?"

"Training is different than reality," the Asuran Prince hissed, "and maybe you'd know that if you did anything to help, not just sit there and tell us how to manage the ripples on the pond."

"Us?" A bushy, grey-streaked eyebrow arched in theatrical inquiry. "Vaasuki has joined your protest now?"

"Vaasuki surely feels the same way," he grumbled.

"Yes. But she shares her thoughts with her teacher and trusts *his* wisdom to guide her through it." He eyed Ravan significantly. "Some might say *that's* the place of a student."

"Is *Vaasuki's* sister missing?" the prince asked harshly.

"Ravan, of course, you are right. This is difficult for you." He waved a hand. "Of course, I will help however I can."

"Maybe you can help our scouts find her?" His heart leaped at the idea. *If anyone can overcome the horrors of the jungle, it's the Teacher.*

"Ravan," the old man remonstrated gently, "I cannot go too deep into the aranya. There are beings there who know me. Some might sense me even as I sleep at night under the canopy. If I should call upon my powers while in the jungle?" He shook his head.

"I don't understand!" the Prince exclaimed. "Would that be *so* bad? I say, let them see you! Let these beings—whatever they are—come rushing down upon you. You'd only make the jungle a safer place if you defeated and killed them! And what matter if the realm of Naraka knew of your existence?"

"Defeated all of them at once?" The sage chuckled. "You overestimate my power, my beloved shikshak. And you know our agreement, Ravan." He held up a hand, ticking up his fingers one by one. "I do not cast spells, except in small doses. I do not manifest myself, except to a select few. I could easily be banished from the realm if my presence were widely known. And I don't get directly involved in Narakan politics." He sighed sorrowfully and shook his head. "I wish it were different, my boy. Believe me. To the Prajapatis, I'm a rule breaker. I risk too much already."

Ravan nodded, adopting a submissive mask. Internally, he boiled with questions. *Risk too much?* he wondered. *What is it you even want here? I know your concern would only be for the greater good,* he thought. However irritating his rules were, the Teacher had proven himself a noble being in every way. Ravan would trust the old man with his life.

"Teacher?" he asked tenuously. "If you can't help directly, what *would* you do?"

"Remember when you asked me about mantras that healed the body quickly?"

Ravan nodded. "You told me they were dangerous, complex. I think you called it slippage, that it can damage flesh. You said the knitting together of tissues could drain the body and leave it lifeless."

In a heartbeat, his mind flashed back to the gurukul years ago, the cave deep in the bones of the earth, where the Teacher delivered the most potent lessons to him and Vaasuki. That far from the surface, he could wield his power with a degree of freedom without fear of being detected.

* * *

In his mind's eye, Ravan was seated cross-legged on a carpet of kusha grass, hands on knees. His eyes were closed, but his soul was open, the third eye hovering in and through his being. Unfortunately, he wasn't yet strong enough to project outside and see with this new dimension of his being.

He just felt it. *Was* it. It was his consciousness and nothing more.

The Teacher had said Ravan would begin to view his inner self with finer and finer distinction, recognizing facets and shades of his being he hadn't yet encountered.

"We are infinitely complex," the Teacher was telling them. "You see the diagrams of Narakan bodies in your minds? The veins, arteries, muscles, organs, bones of Asuras and Nagas?"

Vaasuki and Ravan nodded. The Teacher had forced them to discard books years prior. They relied now only on the memory palaces they had constructed in their minds.

"The races have scarcely begun to learn about their bodies," the Teacher continued. "Even the most sophisticated physicians in Swarga, Naraka, and Bhooloka know but a fraction. The firing of impulses in the mind. The growth of our muscles as we train for battle. We understand but a shadow of these things. The magic of the Vedas can help us control, but not understand fully."

Ravan heard him shifting, standing up from his vantage point and pacing the floor as was his custom. Sometimes, the Teacher lunged down to his students' ears, speaking in strange tongues, writing instructions on their skin with his index finger. Sometimes, he disappeared for hours without warning, but if they opened their eyes during meditation, somehow, he always knew.

Ravan struggled with the urge to peek.

"But the emotional dimension?" The Teacher laughed. "The relational? The spiritual? Of these, most know even less. Not the shadow of a shadow. Not the echo of a dream. Most know not what drives a sentient being. The true source of all thoughts. Now. What do *you* think we should do, Ravan, given that truth?"

"Must these things remain unknown? Can we not learn more?"

"Vaasuki, what do you say?" said the sage.

Ravan heard her slither up into a tighter coil, as she did while thinking intensely. He'd almost always seen her in one of her serpentine forms, half-snake half-Narakan or else completely serpent. She only shifted into her fully Narakan form when the Teacher commanded it.

"We should accept it," she'd whispered softly. Ravan shivered. Her voice was always just a touch more sibilant, a bit snakier than was natural. "We should embrace the mystery. In accepting mystery, we can feel the patterns and begin to guide them."

Ravan smiled, anticipating the Teacher's curt dismissal of her answer. Then he felt a sting upon his ear. He flinched with a grimace, and his eyes instinctively snapped open.

"So confident she's the fool and you're the sage, eh?" the Teacher whispered in his ear, so faint Vaasuki could not hear. "Close your eyes and get back inside your head, shikshak!"

And then, "Classic Naga answer," the old man said loudly.

Ravan heard him resume pacing behind them. "Predictable, not entirely untrue. And Ravan? Classic Asuran response; limited, yet not entirely in error."

Not entirely? The Asuran prince bristled, and the Teacher chuckled. "Yes. You are both correct and both wrong. Excellent, Ravan, for pointing out the difference between things that are true and things that are *the truth*. Mahavira, the great Thirthankara sage, was it?"

"His disciple," Ravan muttered proudly. "The Blind Seer, Divakar. I was reading his discourse on *Anekantavada*, Absolutism versus Relativism, just last week."

"Impressive. Yes. Your answer reflects the truth that we can learn, improve, and master a few elements within us. Yet you fail to acknowledge what Vaasuki has seen—that no matter how long and hard we strive to carve out our rules, the stone we carve on has grains we cannot see. The same rule can be interpreted and followed very differently, based on the perspective of the follower. Sometimes, a greater truth is achieved by feeling, not analyzing."

"Could we just get back to magic?" Ravan said, exasperated.

"Right! Right." The Teacher chuckled. "Where were we?"

"Magic and the body," the two students replied in bitter unison.

"Magic. Indeed. As complex as the pools of our minds are, magic is a pool of stupendous depth. A force of infinite dimensions. Yet, the principle is the same as that of any system of learning. To some degree, we can learn to control it."

"Or else we wouldn't even be here," Ravan grumbled.

"Who trounced who in the last contest?" Vaasuki challenged him, smirking.

"The supernatural has its physics," the Teacher intoned, "just as the natural dimension does. Every time you manifest supernatural power in the natural realm, there is an expenditure of energy. This transfer requires a conduit—a person or sometimes a talisman—through which there can be a loss of energy. The more practiced the sorcerer, the finer the talisman, the less drag there is."

"Drag," Ravan echoed, testing the word. "When energy is lost in the transfer."

"Lost through a conduit," the Teacher specified. "When energy is lost in the actual spell, that is different. Perhaps you channel energy to make a flame. The tiredness you feel after you cast a spell is proportionate to the exact amount of energy you draw. But when you apply it, the energy won't just make a flame. There will be a bit of heat before the fire is kindled. This sudden, unnatural change in temperature can cause a slight wind. The same thing happens when you create an illusion, for example, you—"

"You can create an illusion?" Ravan grinned. "I could use that to convince the chef I haven't stolen any samosas."

"Princeling problems," Vaasuki snorted.

"You could," the Teacher chuckled, "but there would be slippage. Heat as you were weaving a spell. The folding of the air. When the supernatural contacts the natural dimension, it takes a very skilled spellcaster to control its effects completely."

"A skilled spellcaster like you?" Ravan asked.

The Teacher chuckled. "Sometimes, yes. Sometimes, even I make mistakes. Most physical processes, for example, are easier than abstract ones. To block an arrow. To open a door. To light a fire. Very simple. Healing a human body, on the other hand, is incredibly complex. Most don't even know what the body is or how it's joined to the *atman,* the individual consciousness. Yet there are spells to separate the body and the atman and then to reforge them. You're not ready to cast, much less control, these. For now, we'll focus on simple ones. . . "

* * *

"Ravan, so I asked you about the accelerated healing of the body. . . " the Teacher repeated.

Ravan was back in his bedroom, with the pain of his wounds searing through the body and the fire of the Teacher's eyes burning into his soul. He nodded confidently and answered the question. He'd learned much in the years since that discussion about magic in the cave. "The slippage can affect the actual tissue. Air pockets that could get caught inside organs. Nerves and muscles forever fashioned aslant." He shuddered. He'd seen the results of careless healing by inexperienced spellcasters on Lanka before. *Like the time Cousin Vikarna tried to heal his favourite hunting hound. I would never want to inflict that on someone.*

"Precisely." The Teacher nodded. "So, it takes great skill and knowledge to heal using magic. You have not studied it. You were wise to not attempt it on yourself. But I can help you."

Ravan stared. "You have that skill?" he said, surprised but also excited. "You could close my wounds?"

"I can do more than close them." The Teacher smiled. "I can make your body whole." He leaned forward abruptly, hands tightening on Ravan's arm. "But I will only do this under two conditions."

"Yes?" the prince said meekly.

"As soon as you're able, you'll set yourself to finding your lost sister."

Ravan sighed expansively. "Thank you, Teacher." A smile spread across his face.

"Ahh? So quick to accept?" The man frowned, bushy eyebrows knitting together above that steady sapphire gaze.

"Ahh. Right. Your second condition." Ravan suppressed an impatient sigh.

"My second condition: when you go, you will take Vaasuki with you."

"I. . . what? But she's. . . you can't be serious."

"She's your *only* fellow shikshak. So why not take her along?"

Ravan set his chin, annoyed. "Name one good reason to take her."

"Well, she's a Naga, for one—"

Here, Ravan flung out a dramatic hand.

"—which means she's a natural in the jungle," the Teacher finished.

"I just survived the Trial," Ravan grumbled, "and went far deeper into the aranya than she ever has."

"Yet another reason—your feeble state."

"You said you were going to heal me, Teacher."

"And then there is the matter of. . . ah." The sage caught himself and went rigid, looking Ravan firmly in the eyes. "Ravan. Listen to me. This is of grave importance. When you agree to my terms, and I heal you, you will not have completely recovered your energy. Your wounds will be gone. But your body will still be weak. You have barely eaten, barely moved, and you've lost a lot of blood in the past two weeks. I cannot erase these facts from the memory of your body. Ravan! Stop fidgeting about and look at me. You are strong, yes. But you will need help when you go out again. Your *fibres* will be knit together. Your body still remembers the exertion you put it through. I am patching a sura wineskin, but I cannot replace the sura wine that has already been spilled."

"But she hates me!" Ravan exclaimed. "Every chance she gets, she provokes me, mocking my people, my family, and Kaala's halls, even Surpanakha. You know what she thinks of us Asuras!" *She says we are savages, but I know the truth.* If it hadn't been for the Devan conquest, the Asuras would have ruled Naraka. Asuras had the most transcendent magic. They had the metals needed for advanced weapons. Ravan's people thought themselves entitled to dominion, according to Vaasuki.

"Interesting you should say she hates you," the Teacher observed calmly when Ravan's fire had petered out. "She says the same of you."

"But I don't hate her! All I do is defend myself!"

"She says the same; she says the same." The wise man nodded, and then, in a most infuriating manner, reached out to take Ravan's hands in his. "Now hold still while I prepare the mantra."

"By Shiva, I don't want her!" Ravan jerked away. "Teacher, we're officially at war with the Nagas. They send *vish*, poison, to our nobles."

The sage shrugged. "Such is the way of all Narakans, as far as I see it. Are Asuras any different?"

"Asuras defend," Ravan hissed. "Nagas attack. By Shiva's third eye, Father's at war with them even now. That's why he missed my entire bloody ascent to twice-born! If it weren't for the Devan conquest, the entire Nagan kingdom would be bent on destroying us. Their queen, Surassaa Nahgrassand, battles us at the head of a great army of wilders and cityers. A great host of viper Nagas, with their bows and venom, and constrictor Nagas, with their dao swords as infantry."

"Let us thank ourselves then," the Teacher muttered dryly, "for the Devan conquest." He gave Ravan a pointed look. "If we desire peace, perhaps we turn to other things. Saving Surpanakha, for example."

"Vaasuki would never—"

"Vaasuki has already agreed to go with you," the Teacher rumbled sharply, anticipating Ravan's final protest.

At that, the walls of the student's fortitude crumbled as he sagged against the pillow. "At least let me be in charge," Ravan muttered weakly, offering his hands for the healing mantra.

"Vaasuki will lead you to your sister. You will lead the rescue."

"But I'm a better tracker than—"

"You are not a better tracker. You should be thankful I consider you a better strategist. She's actually been coming to lessons these last weeks." He grinned bizarrely, abruptly cheerful as Ravan burst into outraged protest; then, he clapped his hands around Ravan's neck and uttered a *shloka*.

प्रभूतवातादि समस्त रोग-
प्रणाशकर्त्रे मुनिवन्दिताय ।
प्रभाकरेन्द्वग्निविलोचनाय
श्री वैद्यनाथाय नमः शिवाय ॥

(I salute that God Shiva,
Who is the king among physicians,
Who cures all deadly diseases,
Who is saluted by great sages,
And to whom the Sun God,
Moon, and God of Fire are eyes.)

It was a beautiful shloka and very rhythmic. As the Teacher chanted, a rush of heat encased Ravan's body, and a fire crawled up his back. To the prince's amazement, it was a fire that emanated icy coolness, stabbing his skin on his back and shoulders like the sharpest of tryasta or three-pointed needles. In his mind's eye, Ravan was once again seated cross-legged on his carpet of kusha grass, hands on knees. His eyes were closed, but his soul was open, the third eye hovering in and through his being. Something scratched against the very fibres of each muscle and nerve, but from the *inside*. Inside every muscle fibre, as if a spiny serpent with a thousand tails was writhing to get out. It was the single most bizarre thing he had ever felt in his young life.

Chapter 13

The Furnace of Their Cruelty

When Harsha awoke, dawn was already breaking, a whisper of grey-washed orange bleeding across the eastern horizon.

The horizon. He was on a hill that thrust up out of the jungle canopy, like a bare, stony island jutting out from the icy seas of the northern Rakshasas. *Those paagala hulks in their porkkappals sail at the peak of winter.*

Not as crazy as Surpanakha and me trying to navigate the aranya, he thought ruefully. He was on the ground, his arms wrenched back around the trunk of a thick neem tree and bound to it by a tough rope. The coarse bark bit into the skin of his arms and back.

What in the name of the ice giants did they do to my shirt? He surveyed his surroundings. *Nothing.* Just a sea of treetops spreading off into the distance.

Surpanakha! Where is Surpanakha? He tried to suppress the panic that welled up in him. *She must be all right,* he assured himself desperately.

Muji, Har Shaa cursed. There was a being across from him, sitting shrouded in the shadows. Then it rippled. There was coiling in the darkness, and the man's torso thrust out towards Harsha into the tenuous light. Suddenly, the Vidyadharan prince understood what he was looking at.

Naga. He felt a surge of relief. *Perhaps we can bargain our way out. The wilder Nagas of the jungle are known to be hostile to outsiders, but at least they are not all allies of the Devas.*

"What have you done with her?" Harsha demanded, adopting a commanding tone. "What have you done with my friend?" *I will get us out of this mess.*

He had an excellent command voice, Harsha did. He'd honed it from a young age under the watchful eyes of his doting father, Chitraketu, the king of the Vidyadharas. The peak-dwellers of the sapta kula, the seven tribes, bowed to their Lords but they were not known to bend the knee to just anyone. Harsha was well versed in the laws of power—how authority was captured or cultivated. How to create a mirage of power where none existed.

The illusion of power can accomplish a great deal, his father would say. *Many a tyrant, many a rebel has kept control through the mere appearance of strength.*

With this particular Naga, however, my command voice seems to have little effect. Instead, there was a stirring in the shadows, a shrugging of broad shoulders, and then, the Naga disappeared into the dark. Then, he transformed.

It was a bizarre sight, the massive serpent's body broadening gradually into the bare upper torso of an average male. *Midform, they call it.* His chest was nearly as broad as a Rakshasa's, his hair a wild mass of thick, black curls that tumbled to his shoulders. He wore no clothing whatsoever but clutched a curved dagger in one hand.

Harsha suppressed a shudder. Sharing their climes in the equatorial lowlands of Naraka, Surpanakha accepted the Nagas as somewhat natural. However, for a Vidyadhara, there would always be something too savage—unnatural—about the hybrid races.

Shakti created us to be of Nature. But not to be mingled with the animals. Not to be joined with those we hunt.

"My name," the Naga said, "is Wajra-Danssh."

"Wajra-Danssh." Harsha nodded coolly. "What have you done with the girl?"

"She will be safe," the Naga replied, "so long as you behave. So long as you *both* behave." He paused meaningfully. "She has been rebellious so far. . . "

"She's *awake?* Let me see her at once! If you have hurt her—"

"You will see her," Wajra-Danssh interrupted.

He's unlike any Nagan savage I've heard of. Nothing like the bloodthirsty illiterates from the stories told by the sapta kulas of the Peaks.

"She had to be bound and forced unconscious." Wajra-Danssh shrugged regretfully. "She lacks your poise and common sense, I must say."

She lacks my cowardice, Harsha thought bitterly, straining at the rope that cut into his wrists. *If only I had no crown. No duty. Then I could abandon all thought and fling myself against the hybrids in rabid hatred.*

As best as one can fling oneself while bound, he thought, giving up with a sigh as his wrists began to bleed from the useless effort. "You knocked the girl unconscious?" *When I'm free, I will brand you a dozen times for every glance you cast her way, haraami.* "Why didn't you wake me? I could have calmed her with a word."

Wajra-Danssh arched an eyebrow in bemusement. "What is your name, Vidyadhara?"

"I am Harsha of the Ishaavni Mountain Gurungs."

The Naga blinked but appeared otherwise unimpressed. Harsha couldn't say whether he recognized the name or not.

"Are you always this calm, Harsha of the Ishaavni Mountain Gurungs?"

"I had it burned into me. Forged through years of guidance from the harshest teachers. Such discipline is needed to rule."

"To rule?" At last, the man betrayed emotion, a flickering of amusement. "You have no idea how many prisoners try that. Some promise of coin or other rewards. Swearing that they are noble. Threats of revenge. Rakshasas promise us command over the tides. A few Asuras have insisted they have access to some magic plant named *soma* that helps with spellcasting." He chuckled. "But I'm afraid we are powerless in this matter, my friend. We have our orders."

"But I *am* Harsha, Prince of the Vidyadharas!" he said, mind racing. *Shakti, give me strength.* "I swear it! Take me to my father, and you shall be richly rewarded. At least send spies to confirm what I'm saying! That should be enough to—"

"Enough!" Wajra-Danssh interrupted, "I am responsible for my crew's survival. We will trade for you with the Devas."

"The *Devas!*" Harsha spat. "The Devas are the ones that damned this land!" *Of course.* Wilder Nagan savages would have killed them on sight if angered or dropped from the trees to give them a simple warning that they had strayed near village land. Few ventured deep into the aranya. Everybody knew—the Nagas didn't take prisoners.

As all beasts, he remembered Father saying. *They lack a proper understanding of sapient nature. Of psychological manipulation, of bargaining with lives.*

"You work for the *Devas,*" Harsha hissed in horror. They hadn't been captured by mere Nagan wilders—they'd been captured by bloody slavers. *Traitors! And you seemed so understanding. I thought perhaps we'd stumbled on to your land. I thought we had a chance at freedom.*

"Indeed." The sorrow in Wajra-Danssh's eyes seemed genuine. "I do what I can to preserve my people. But if you are a prince,"—he paused—"and I think you might be—then you know this most of all."

"If you think I'm a prince," Harsha grated, "then let us go! Imagine the consequences for Naraka. For all the races!"

"And would you let me go if our positions were reversed?" the Naga challenged.

There was a brief pause as shouting flared up somewhere off through the trees, a chorus of angry curses followed by a high-pitched shriek. *That's Surpanakha!*

"It seems your friend is awake," Wajra-Danssh observed dryly. A moment later, a spitting, thrashing Surpanakha was thrust into the clearing by a train of Nagan warriors in midform. They flung her down and surrounded her, watching impassively as she scrambled to her feet, practically spitting fire.

"She is indeed awake," Wajra-Danssh said. "And very beautiful. That's good for her. For both of you." He clicked his tongue, looking Harsha up and down and humming an idle tune. "In fact, I find both of you quite striking. I'm not one to predict Indra's tastes, of course, but I do wager that you'll both end up quite nicely, if—"

"*Ahallika! Bastards*" Surpanakha spat from behind him. "Vampire of Demoness Aran Yani! Harsha, did you know they work for *Indra?* These idiots have got their forked tongues so far up his cold-bloode—"

"Surpanakha! Be quiet! That's no way to bargain with our captors."

"*Bargain?*" Surpanakha barked. "You think I'm going to bargain with these *daasya putras*? No. You, barrel chest." She jerked a chin towards Wajra-Danssh. "Bring me your leader."

"Surpanakha!" Harsha strained against his bonds, twisting in a vain attempt to meet her gaze. "Don't call them—"

"No, no, no." The Naga's voice was eerily grave.

As if he sympathizes with Surpanakha, Harsha thought.

"It's quite natural that she should feel such anger. We are, after all, your captors." He shifted in the darkness, face fading in and out of light.

"The consequences, Wajra-Danssh!" Harsha urged. "Imagine my father's rage. Imagine the anger of our kingdoms *combined!*"

"I'll let the Devas decide whether to believe you or not. We all think first of those dearest to us, Harsha of the Ishaavni Gurungs. As a ruler, you protect your loved ones best by keeping your family in power, by keeping your kingdom stable. In my case, however. . . " his lips twisted with a bitter smile, "if I let you go, they would flay my wife. They would slice up my *children.* My warriors' wives and *their* children. They would make me watch. After that horror, perhaps they'd give me a quick death. No, Harsha! I obey the Devas. They have built a world of iron and fire. If I disobeyed, I'd just be another imperfection burned away in the furnace of their cruelty."

"You speak of them as enemies, yet you do their bidding," Harsha spat.

A second Naga came slithering from the darkness, twining its coils around Harsha's helpless figure. "Surely you've heard of free Nagan slavers?"

"Enough, Musssaan," Wajra-Danssh warned, nudging the snake away. "These are victims of necessity. Of fate and Devan cruelty. They are not our foes."

Harsha experienced this strange feeling that he would have actually *liked* Wajra-Danssh if they'd met under better circumstances.

That will make it all the more a pity to kill the bastard.

"I speak of them as enemies yet do their bidding. Yes. Are you any different?" Wajra-Danssh laughed loudly. "You nobles and your endless fawning? What of the tribute you drag from your people just to keep Devan longswords at bay? You take grain and coin from peasants and fishermen, the very warp and weft of their survival. And for what? To retain your marble floors. Your soaring vaulted ceilings. Your idols of Ratnapur turquoise adorned with gold."

Harsha was swiftly beginning to re-evaluate his appreciation for Wajra-Danssh's 'honourable' sincerity.

Then the Naga sighed, and this time, Harsha felt anger simmering deep within the Naga leader. "Do not lecture me, Vidyadhara, on what is courage and what is folly. We do what we must to protect ourselves and those we love. The only difference is you were born with power enough that the Devas grafted you into their system. They use you to collect their taxes and take what they need from the land. On the other hand, I am so insignificant that I would simply disappear without consequence if I were to betray them. So, keeping your value to your people in mind. . . " his tail curled out to weave between Surpanakha and Harsha, a living wall of scaled flesh, "I can offer you a way out. I currently hold two slaves. Get me more, and I shall set you free."

Harsha blinked. "What? What exactly do you think a prince does for his people?"

"You are wise. Skilful. Come now, Vidyadhara." Wajra-Danssh's voice was soothing. "You would give yourself up for your people, wouldn't you? Why not let them sacrifice for you? Get me, say. . . seven Asuras. Seven Vidyadharas. Yes, seven of each for the iron mine in this jungle." He lifted a casual hand. "Nothing, in the grand scheme of things. Nothing to save a prince. Get me fourteen others, and I promise you shall—"

"May your fangs rot in hell, *paapis!*" Surpanakha shouted.

"Mmm. Unfortunate." As his men bundled Surpanakha to the ground and jammed a gag into her mouth, Wajra-Danssh turned to Musssaan, motioning for Harsha to be untied. "And you, Vidyadhara? You seem open to reason."

"I couldn't have said it any better," Harsha hissed. "May your fangs rot in hell, *haraami!" An iron mine? Are the Devas using slaves to mine ayas in the jungle? But why haven't our pisachas ever seen the mine? The Devas must have warded off the entire mine from above with their evil Brahmaic white magic!*

A flurry of blows landed on his face and body. Wajra-Danssh's men pounded him with feverish hatred until the Naga leader ordered them to stop.

"Untie him and get him marching," the Naga ordered. "We'll get them to the Devan mine and they'll learn their lesson soon enough."

The thing Harsha hated most as they hoisted him up and prodded him with iron spear tips was that Wajra-Danssh's eyes held a deep sorrow. *This man really hates what he does, but he does it for his crew.*

Don't care if he empathizes. I'll kill them all, Harsha swore. *I will drown their children in blood for every scratch they put on Surpanakha, the dalaals.*

The hours passed slowly, a melange of visceral despair and anger, mingled with a fierce but vague resolve. *Somehow, sometime, the opportunity for escape will present itself. And when it does. . .*

Brightest was the fear, nightmarish and vivid. They were being taken to a Devan iron mine, and not a soul knew where they were. *Father and the Asuras might pick up our trail, but we'll have disappeared by then.* When Wajra-Danssh suggested they were beautiful and sophisticated enough to serve in Indra's palace, the Naga slaver had meant it as a kindness. To Harsha, there was no greater dread. To pass through the icy northern Kshirada seas to Swarga, the realm of the Devas, was to sever the cord completely, to plummet off the brink with no hope of return.

Surpanakha echoed his fears in the scattered minutes they were permitted conversation. "To be taken from our realm," she sobbed. They were sitting bound to a tree, back to back in the centre of the slaver camp. The Nagas coiled in the branches all around them. The grove echoed with the whispering, rustling, slithering of their massive serpentine bodies through the trees. It was a nightly routine. Still, Harsha found it keenly unnerving.

"Uncle Akampana says Swarga, the realm of the Devas, is dead," Surpanakha whispered in the darkness. "Lightless. Especially the north, where Indra rules from his capital, Amaravati. Rain falls as ice. The winds are soulless. They say Swargan forests have no pulse, no warmth."

"I know," Harsha murmured softly, straining against the ropes. He wished he could wrap his arms around her.

"I know," he repeated. "Don't worry. Shakti watches us, and Shiva, too. They will not lead us to doom."

"How could they have let this happen to us?" she wept.

Goddess Chamundi, give me faith. Surpanakha's family was more practical than pious. "The Gods are in everything," the

Vidyadharan prince urged. "Their eyes are on every creature, their breath in every breeze. We cannot walk upon a path that Shiva and Shakti don't guard." *Please, Surpanakha.* Now more than ever, he needed her to believe.

"If this is the Gods guarding us," she spat, "then I want nothing of it. Swarga, Harsha! They are taking us to *Swarga!*"

"I won't let that happen," Harsha swore. "Whatever it takes, Surpanakha, I will see you freed. I won't rest until I've found a way."

There was a sharp hiss from the trees, warning them to be silent. Harsha settled down, retreating into the darkness of his thoughts.

And so, the hours passed, each drawing them closer to the Devan mine and a lifetime of captivity. Harsha snatched what moments he could of conversation with Surpanakha, but they were few and harried. *Each time, she sounds more. . . frail. Jagged.* The dread haunted them both, but within him, it seeded grim determination. In her, it was welling swiftly into a panic.

Harsha's uncle, Shukla Yudhaana, Warrior of the Morning Mist, had trained him to recognize the signs. *It is at the far fringe of despair that we plunge into insanity,* he had once said. *We can cower before our affliction or take courage and give ourselves entirely to battle. Madness is inevitable for those who sink into the morass of gloom.*

And so, they drifted, each battling their inner demons. It was torture for Harsha to see his priyatama prodded by their spears, bleeding from the sores on her wrists and ankles from the ropes. Wajra-Danssh maintained his gentility and honour without flaw, but a few of the Naga slavers delighted in tormenting the teenagers. The pair were spat on, kicked, and even beaten as their leader slept.

For three nights, Musssaan proved the worst. He was a violent bully when Wajra-Danssh wasn't around, feared by the others. He would wake in the dead of night and slither in serpent form to where the prisoners sat bound, encircling their tree and coiling down in ever-smaller circles. The sentries let him do as he wished, and some even joined in with relish.

Harsha, they largely ignored, but against Surpanakha, they brushed their scales, first across her legs and then slowly up her body, hissing with pleasure as she struggled to shrink from their touch. On the first night it happened, she snarled and spat in fury, but then quieted with a whimper when Musssaan constricted abruptly around Harsha, binding his chest with such strength that the Vidyadhara could barely breathe. The jungle began to swim before Harsha's eyes, lungs straining fruitlessly for breath.

"Sssssubmit," the Naga whispered, "or your princeling diesssss."

As Surpanakha relented with a sob, the Naga hissed with satisfaction and continued his exploration of her body with his coils. "Not a ssssound," he hissed. "Not a whissssper. Or I shall kill you both this very night."

This persisted the next two nights. Harsha was petrified by fear and indecision. Then, finally, he could take no more and let loose a single shout one night.

"Bassstard!" Musssaan hissed, sliding over to Harsha quicker than a heartbeat and wrapping his coils around the teen. For the first time, the Vidyadhara appreciated how powerful a fully grown Nagan constrictor was. The darkness of the night flickered into a distant blur, and his heartbeat thundered in his ears. Unarmed and without his pisacha, he was nothing before this creature. A mere mouse in the talons of a Kinnaran hunting falcon.

Harsha felt his consciousness begin to fade as his mind went mad for air, and then simply began to drift away. . .

"*Bassstard!* Now you di—"

There was a flash of writhing motion, a hiss of sound, and the Naga's form went limp. Breath returned in a rush, the sweetest thing Harsha had ever tasted. Wajra-Danssh rose from Musssaan's still form, hissing with displeasure. His serpentine figure *rippled,* and the man stepped out. The transformation was nearly instantaneous. One moment there was a serpent before him, and the next, a man.

Harsha had never seen a being so furious. "The prisoners are NOT to be touched!" Wajra-Danssh roared. "Look to Musssaan's corpse and see his folly."

All around them, the wilder Nagas coiled, cowering in submission.

"Does anyone else wish to disobey me?" Wajra-Danssh spread his arms in invitation. "I stand before you naked. Fangless. And welcome any comer!"

Silence.

"And you," Wajra-Danssh turned to the lone voiceless sentry, coiled around a tree at some distance. "You sat by and watched this?"

"Lord," the creature grovelled, "you know Musssaan. He threatened to kill my children. He knows my village. He—"

"If any of you undermines me," Wajra-Danssh spat, "I shall have his head. I shall burn him on Vritra's altar and see his ashes fed to my pet eels. He shall have no place in Vritra's halls."

The harassment ceased after that, but tension of a darker nature emerged. The slavers were bitterly divided. Some detested

Musssaan as a bully. Others resented his death, and those muttered against Wajra-Danssh when his back was turned.

"An Asuran wench has no honour in Vritra's eyes," a slaver spat at Surpanakha one night when Wajra-Danssh was away. "I spare you now because I fear him. Because he's the highest of the slavers. But Musssaan was a Naga true. No true-blood Naga should be sacrificed for the non-existent honour of an Asuran *thethenumaa,* a whore."

Harsha almost felt relief when they reached the ridge overlooking their destination. Below them was a clearing vast enough to hide ten villages of his people. The slopes of the hills around the clearing had been stripped of all vegetation. *Desolate,* he thought. Massive faces of layered granite, broken by reddish-orange land, thrust forth from the ground, scarred by the marks of the Devas. Pulleys, ladders, and tiny forms of hundreds of sentient beings clung to the sides. *They're as tiny as people appear when I look down upon them from the back of my beloved Uluka.*

Coarse wooden towers protruded from the jungle floor, manned by sentries carrying massive halberds. An array of huge black instruments of some sort dotted the valley floor like so many twisted monstrosities of metal and wood. Shafts, pulleys, levers, and wheels worked by slaves turning huge wheels. The smell of burning coal wafted up to where they stood, and it twisted his stomach with disgust.

A welcome party issued from the gates below—Devan warriors with tall halberds and shining, chain-mail armour. "Today, your fate will be determined," Wajra-Danssh said gravely. "I'm afraid I can help you no longer. You are strong. Intelligent. You could do well in Indra's courts—but you *must* learn submission." He turned to Surpanakha. "Look to Harsha's wisdom. Bow your head and look away, and you shall surely earn favour. There must be *no* open resistance. Bide your time. Serve them well. If the master prospers, so too does the slave."

Harsha scowled, suppressing a shudder of revulsion. *The Naga is right.* Surpanakha was silent.

The Naga sighed. His shoulders slumped. "If you wish," he relented, "I shall tell them of your royal blood. That I believe you. They may consider negotiation." He did not need to voice his doubt; it was apparent in the hollowness of his tone. "But before we part, one thing." His voice held the deep sorrow of a man long acquainted with shame. "You should know that there was no version of this in which I could have freed you. Indra sees all. He knows all." He gestured over a shoulder to his group of slavers. "The Devas only let me live because I am the best there is. No one catches slaves better, and no one commands obedience as I. If I were to stop. . . " he shook his head, ". . . there are others waiting to take my place."

Harsha stifled the anger that welled up within him. *Justice. Honour. Courage.* They mattered not in a world ruled by Devas. *Someday, I will learn how this man was cursed with his life. Right before I drive my bichuwa into his heart.* Wanly, the prince said, "Let's go then."

Chapter 14

A Song of Weeping

All thoughts of escape during the handover vanished from Harsha's mind as the Devan reception party emerged. Two dozen warriors they sent out, surrounding the slavers in a ring. Wajra-Danssh was paid in silver *rupyarupa* coins, his stores of meat and water replenished. The Nagan slaver shared a few words with the tall, fair-haired warriors. Then, Wajra-Danssh turned and disappeared into the steamy aranya at the head of his wilder Nagas.

Harsha had seen no sign of his pisacha, Uluka, during their captivity in the jungle. *For millennia, Nagas have employed thermal sensing and stealth to avoid jungle predators,* he thought. *If Uluka had passed above, he couldn't have seen us through the jungle canopy, forget tracking us through the winding trails Wajra-Danssh used.* The Vidyadharan prince refused to consider the alternative, that his bond mate lay dead somewhere high up in the vast canopy of the aranya.

But Harsha had clung to the vain hope that his beloved pisacha, bonded to him for life, would emerge at the handover point and help them escape. Upon seeing the Devan forces and the security of the complex, however, that hope quickly faded.

"It will be impossible to escape now," he muttered to Surpanakha, regretting the words the moment they left his mouth.

"Forgive me." His lip quivered. "It's just. . . Uluka was our best hope. I thought he might follow us somehow and come swooping down with his mighty talons to set us free. I was a *moorkha,* a fool. Right after our capture was the time for action, when we might have escaped under cover of the jungle."

"No, my beloved, my priyatama." Surpanakha's hand found his own when they were finally allowed to sit on the straw-strewn floor of a cave carved into the hillside. The vastness of the mine spread out before them, visible through the iron bars of the gate that barred the entrance to the cave.

It was a dismal sight. Endless terraced layers of naked earth stretched for *yojanas* across the valley, the colour of lifeless rust. The valley floor was dotted with an array of machines, writhing monstrosities of iron and wood and smoke. It looked like a scar in the centre of the beautiful jungle made by a Kinnaran *talwar. An enormous, curved blade thrust into Naraka's beating heart.*

The mine occupied a vast valley rimmed to the east and west by small but steep-sloped hills. Crowning the valley to the north was a majestic hill. Where the eastern and western slopes were overgrown with low brush—the trees on those had seemingly been cleared decades earlier—the northern hill, like the heart of the mine itself, was naked granite.

It was in a cave on the slope of this hill that Surpanakha and Harsha were now held. A pair of Devan guards had deposited them on the floor of the cave, which was about halfway up the hill. The two teens hobbled over to the bars of the iron gate that held them, rubbing the circulation back into their limbs and whispering to one another as they studied their new home.

"So many," Surpanakha's voice trembled, "I had no idea." The slope swarmed with tiny forms, forlorn and nearly naked beneath the pitiless sun as they plodded through the desolation. Despite the distance, Harsha could discern the straining of their limbs and the grim, dogged strides with which they shoved their carts, swung their picks, or urged the teams of buffalo that carried their loads up a massive central path. He could almost imagine the twisted agony on their faces.

As they contemplated the dismal scene, Harsha came to appreciate just how forgiving Wajra-Danssh had been. The Devan overseers wielded their flails more cheerily than Vidyadharan Ojha priestesses their ball-chains of incense at the temples of his beloved Peaks.

They seemed about three hundred in number, the overseers—not including the fair-haired Devas who stood watch upon every lofty wooden tower that lined the formidable palisade. *Looks like thirty towers,* he thought. *That makes roughly four hundred in all. Wonder how many others are in the barracks.*

He blinked, realizing Surpanakha was speaking. "You were wise, my love. Wajra-Danssh's men were guarding us too closely for us to attempt an escape. Remember what he said? 'There's not a captive that doesn't think to escape while they're still in the jungle.' He had those godless Nagan *naastika* bastards watching our every move. Vijaatas!.."

"Look around us, Surpanakha!" He made a futile gesture towards the bars that sealed them in. Towards the endless stretch of ravaged earth that crawled with Devan overseers. "I'd sooner try to sneak into the caves of Dundubhi with that mountain's wild pisachas and giant migoi apes than. . . " He sighed, bowing his head to rest upon the iron bars. "I'm sorry, my love. Forgive me. I swear that I will see us free." *Paagal! See the way she trembles? See the red of unshed tears upon her face? She hid them from you because you are weak. You are a fool and a coward. If she cannot share her fears with you, who can she turn to?*

"I will see us free," he swore, this time with fervour.

"I believe you, my love." She shifted closer and pressed herself against him, her head on his naked chest, both filthy from hours of endless trekking. "I believe you."

The Devan commander was a tall man, his striking hair the pale, golden colour of ripe wheat. Garbed in the manner of Devas on Naraka, he wore a light cotton tunic, supple but tight-fitting leather breeches, knee-high boots, and a belt of leather from which hung an impressive, gleaming basket-hilted longsword. In addition, he wore a cape, like all high-ranking Devas, emblazoned with the lightning symbol of Indra's personal Vajra brigade. It was light and filmy, adapted from the traditional Devan cut to match the steamy climate of the jungle. His eyes were a startling green, a mark of demon blood. Harsha had heard a rumour somewhere that the Devas were bred with demons to produce an even stronger species but had never seen evidence of it until that moment.

The lovers were locked in conversation when he appeared outside the cave backed by a trio of guards carrying iron-tipped halberds, who glared at them menacingly.

The Vidyadharan prince scrambled to his feet as the gate was unlocked. His fists were clenched, and his jaw was set, but his legs quivered in nervous anticipation. "Hello," he said. *If captured,* Father whispered in his mind, *make sure you set the tone of the relationship. Grasp what power you can, however minor, and stretch it as far as you are able. Put on a facade of confidence if nothing else.*

The commander arched a straw-coloured eyebrow. "I am Maragat-Akash, commander of these forces of Chakravarthi Indra, and superintendent or akaradhyaksha of the Ayasapur mine."

He gestured behind him, a careless motion that encompassed the vastness of the mine, slave, overseer, and soldier alike. A massive silver ring set with a round emerald flashed on the third finger of his right hand. "I certainly don't come in person to welcome every filthy slave that arrives here, but Wajra-Danssh informed me through my men that you were of note." He finished with a smile Harsha did not like at all.

"I. . . " Harsha bowed meekly. "Harsha Gurung of the Ishaanvi—"

"Do hush." The Devan sighed. "Typically, my men would have seen to your cleaning and feeding." He motioned at their filthy state. "The slaver said you comported yourselves with honour, and I dislike welcoming honourable souls in such a manner. Even slaves."

"That is commendable," Harsha said, investing the words with conviction.

"We are all but facets of Lord Brahma's harmonious creation." The Devan shrugged his impressive shoulders. "We must play our parts, yet that does not mean we cannot do so with dignity. Do you not agree?" The large gate groaned open, and he gestured, inviting them outside.

Harsha followed, grateful for the chance to move around. "Indeed." *Could this be a second Wajra-Danssh? Could Goddess Chamundi have blessed us so?*

"Just one thing." Maragat-Akash flicked a hand, and three halberd butts smashed into Harsha's gut. He was slammed against the iron grate and pinned there for a moment as he battled for breath. Surpanakha's screams seemed to drift over the air in a wave, oddly distant through the thundering in his ears.

One of the guards reached out, cuffing him cruelly on the ear as all three withdrew their weapons. Harsha collapsed gasping on the reddish stones that paved the cave, reaching for Surpanakha as they advanced upon her. *Not her, you haraamis!* A tortured snarl ripped from his throat. *Not her!* She staggered and fell as they bludgeoned her, a halberd-butt in the stomach and another cracking across her cheekbone. Her head snapped sideways, and she stumbled, collapsing atop him.

"Bastards!" he croaked. "Haraamis! What did we ever do—" The butt of a halberd smashed into his jaw, smashing his head against the bars and filling his mouth with blood.

"Wajra-Danssh mentioned something else," the commander commented. The soldiers seized Harsha by his long hair, dragging him to his feet. Surpanakha was yanked up beside him. Her terrified whimpers sent shards of black ice slicing through his soul.

Twin quillon daggers were pressed against their throats. "He mentioned you claimed to be of royal blood. Both of you." The Deva grinned coldly and performed a mocking bow. "It would be an honour to receive royals at Ayasapur, I must say. However, I know this must be inaccurate. Can you tell me why?" His green eyes glittered, deadly.

"The Accords," Surpanakha muttered thickly, a trickle of blood running from her lips. Tears tracked pale streaks through the grime and blood that smeared her beautiful face. "They forbid any of the races entering this section of the jungle."

"Yes, the Accords forbid Narakans from entering the heart of this miserable aranya." Maragat-Akash nodded. "Which would indeed include this mine. Your companion here reeks of the distant mountains; him I might have possibly forgiven. But you?" His fingers drifted up to brush her cheek, stroking the gentle curve of her jaw.

Harsha's blood began to boil. "Are you not of the Asuras, my little beauty?"

Maragat sighed as Surpanakha strained in desperate futility, back against the iron grate, jaw clenched in a hopeless attempt at courage. "Do stop struggling, child. It only arouses my men. Just answer the question. You are Asuran?"

"I am." She raised her chin. "I am Surpanakha, daughter of Maharaja Vishravasura of Asurapura, heiress to the Second Throne."

"As I said." The Deva shook his blonde head in feigned sorrow. "Royalty. A common *jada,* an idiot, I might forgive this trespass, but you? Indeed—if memory serves—it was the Asuran royal house which not only signed the Accords with Indra first but also won the other races to the table. Was it not?"

"A fact I deem our greatest shame," said the princess.

Shakti save us. "Surpanakha!" Harsha flinched as Maragat smiled. An evil grin.

"Is that so?" The Devan commander's voice was cold as the bichuwa of a Vidyadharan assassin, thrust through the ear into the brain. "Is it a shame to unite your people and ensure their safety? To herald in a greater age of Lord Brahma's light and understanding?"

"If this is Brahma's light," Surpanakha snarled, "then I prefer to languish in Kaala's dark—"

"Surpanakha!" Harsha snapped as a quillon cut against his throat, drawing blood. "Let me speak, by the Goddess! She's blabbering from fright. We've been days without a proper meal. Surpanakha, listen to me. You need to stay calm."

"Yes." The Devan commander nodded. "Hearken to the wisdom of your long-haired companion. Royalty must understand when to defy and when to bow. To trespass in an area forbidden by your conquerors would be most foolish. It would be a crime against Indra. And the blame would fall on both your races. It would cause distrust. War. Unimaginable chaos. What do you think, men? Do you suppose a true noble of the Vidyadharas would ever do such a thing?"

The tall, fair-haired soldiers chuckled.

"See?" Maragat grinned cheerily. "So you can't be royals, can you?" If you were"—his smile vanished in an instant—"I'd have to declare the Accords null and void. The mighty forces of Chakravarthi Indra would march upon your people after a declaration of war."

"You wouldn't." Harsha winced as the dagger bit ever so slightly into the softness of his throat. Its sting was bright and crisp. "You need the Accords."

Maragat sighed, rolling his eyes heavenward and muttering a prayer in Sanskrit. "Release them." He waved a hand to his men, and they stepped away, daggers dropping to their hips but still clutched at the ready. Harsha and Surpanakha sagged against the iron gate, gasping for breath.

"Let me speak frankly if you truly are that slow. You have violated the Accords. Were you nobles, that would be a gesture of unimaginable defiance. Were I to free you, it would encourage a spark of rebellion amongst the slaves. Your peoples might even seek revenge against Indra. The consequences would be catastrophic for Naraka." He grinned. "Now, we could mitigate this, of course, with some sort of punishment. Slaughtering a number of the slaves, perhaps, and then demanding more. Perhaps five hundred Vidyadharas, five hundred Asuras. More overseers in Lanka. . . your families under constant observation. Perhaps we would double taxes. There would be a myriad of possibilities."

He paused, eyes twinkling. "But the damage would be irreversible. You would have spat in the face of Chakravarthi Indra—and while the spilling of Narakan blood might assuage us momentarily, it would make you martyrs. The seed of rebellion never truly dies, and this might nourish it to sprouting. No matter the punishment I exact, the tension between our peoples would grow. I cannot have that. Do you understand?"

Goddess Kali strike this dalaal down where he stands, Harsha prayed fervently, refusing to meet the commander's gaze. *I know where this is going.*

"Do you understand?" The powerful Deva lashed out with a fist, his ring striking Harsha on the temple.

The world reeled around the teen prince, a whirlwind of colours and dizzying shadow. Surpanakha was screaming far above him, pleading for mercy. "We understand!" she sobbed. "We understand! Please, just stop."

"So! You see?" By the time Harsha's mind cleared, the Devan had polished his silver ring clean of blood, the emerald gleaming softly in the sunlight that filtered in through a crack in the cave ceiling. "Even if I did believe you—and I don't—there could be no royals here. In this place, you are merely chattel, two more among hundreds."

"And if we are telling the truth?" Harsha rasped from where he lay, pressing a hand gingerly to his bleeding temple. "What do you think will happen?"

The Devan shrugged most eloquently. "The princess of Asuras and the prince of Vidyadharas missing?" He shook his head mournfully. "How sad. How very, very sad. Into the heart of the aranya, you say? Mmm, tragic indeed. A foolish choice. Everyone knows the centre of the aranya is forbidden. All sorts of nasty beasts and strange magics, you know. *Videzhiya,* creatures that transcend this world, roam free here. Such foolish children. You'd expect more wisdom from Narakan royal houses." He shrugged in theatrical sorrow, his eyes twinkling with silent laughter. "Such a tragedy. I wonder what took them. A simurgh, perhaps? A river makara? Hmmm, maybe a bhramari, a giant bee!"

"The Gods will give us vengeance," Harsha swore, curling his fingers into bloody fists as the guards heaved him up onto his feet.

The man chuckled. "The Gods? Which Gods, Vidyadhara? We've ruled your land for centuries, and your Gods stand by in silence. If they exist at all, it seems they've bowed to Brahma's greater power. Accept your fate, mountain boy. The Creator weaves all things in harmony. Now begone." He motioned to his guards. "Take them away and see them clothed. Then give them to overseer Haandi."

It was a humiliating process. First, Harsha and Surpanakha were stripped and doused with frigid water. The men took particular delight with Surpanakha, scrubbing ruthlessly until the cuts on her face cracked open. The blood ran fresh down the curve of her throat, her breasts, and down to the nakedness between her thighs.

Harsha could only watch and tremble in silence, knowing that whatever he did would only make it worse. But he was beginning to learn. Victory might be impossible, but complete submission might transform defeat into something bearable.

Submit, then, Harsha thought, *until an opening for victory appears. I will not let Surpanakha die here, the Chausathi Yogini Goddesses help me. I will not allow us to live here a single week longer than necessary.*

But for now, he could only stand and watch as the tall, pale-haired guards ran their hands over Surpanakha's naked body, leering and chuckling and pawing with their large, hungry hands. Prajapati Manu LawGiver's rules forbade taking her if she were a royal. Still, they took joy in making their appetites quite clear.

Fortunately for everyone involved, Harsha thought darkly. If they had come so much as a finger's breadth closer to violating his priyatama, he would have seen them dead in a heartbeat. Even if it meant his own death.

When they were both cleaned and their clothes burned, they were offered slave garb, little more than rust-coloured rags woven with a black hammer, the sign of their future overseer, Haandi.

And so they found themselves thrust into work not hours after they arrived at the Devan mine. It was torture. Simple enough but as grueling as anything Harsha had ever done. Over the following span of days—he lost track of how many—he began to lose all thoughts of defiance, much less escape.

He thought only of survival. Of the cool mud of the slave pens at night and the blessed sleep it brought. Of avoiding the hot bite of the lash and the halberds of the Devan soldiers. Countless hours he passed beneath the brutal sun, pushing endless ore carts from the diggings to the furnaces. And day by day, he only felt himself grow weaker.

The mine was more or less divided into two. The northern section—the one just beneath the miniature mountain, where Maragat's private chambers and several other, lesser caves were carved—was upriver and housed the people of the mine, both slave and Devan. At the eastern flank of Maragat's hill, there was a gate in the stockade. The gate opened up to fields that had been cleared for buffalo to graze. From there ran a central road through the heart of the mine, dividing the barracks from the slave pens and then piercing the centre of the massive holes in the reddish earth for some several hundred metres until it curled westward towards the primary gate. From there, it opened out to the road by which Harsha and Surpanakha had arrived and which, he could now be sure, joined a network that spanned the whole of Devan-occupied Naraka.

The three-thousand-odd slaves were cramped into ten massive pens of iron, crude but emphatically fashioned structures, patrolled at night by no less than a dozen guards each. To their east—farthest from the barracks—were the buffalo pens. A steady rotation of the hapless creatures was kept ready for work while the others grazed outside the mine. Separating the pens from the tunnels were the furnaces, where the ayas ore was smelted and the iron refined. And on the other side, just a bowshot over the road, were the sprawling barracks.

Harsha came to loathe the tunnels. It was torture.

Back and forth, back and forth. Every trip was a nightmare of backbreaking agony. In mere hours, it began to rule Harsha's world—that rhythm of ore and sun and swimming anguish. He passed Surpanakha occasionally on the trail, her cart laden lighter than his, but he could see that her torment was just as unrelenting. The overseers knew their work well, pressing each slave to their individual limits.

Haandi was a filthy swine of a man, a Rakshasan giant who hailed from the icy islands to the north. In the opportunistic manner typical to cowards and bullies, he had cast off all honour and loyalty when he arrived in the Devan mine. It seemed a common enough pattern among crew leaders; common labourers whispered of it with a mingling of envy and disgust.

"Two years licking Devan boots," one ragged woman croaked to Harsha. "The slightest talk of resentment among the slaves, and he'd turn his own mother in. They could share blood—hell, they could be from the same bloody island—and he'd still sell them out. He'd turn us in for even looking at a Deva too long. He'd paint insubordination where there was none, just to seem the hero." She spat and shook her head, cursing as they toiled up the final hill before the compound. The day's work was finished. They were afforded quick conversations as they trailed back for dinner, which consisted of stale bajra chapati—bread made from millets—and rice gruel.

But they had to be wary, even in conversation amongst themselves. Everywhere prowled the overseers, wielding their five-tailed whips. Harsha learned quite intimately that the lashes were not as ordinary as they'd appeared from the cavern cell. The ends were woven with tiny shards of glass, too small to cause actual injury but large enough to lay a thousand little slices across an errant back.

He could not see the lines on his own back, of course, but he saw many upon the backs of others. Long, tangled lines weeping crimson, coated by a thick layer of the all-pervasive dust of the mine. It was a fine powder, red-orange in colour, covering naked limbs and chests until the slaves seemed to be a thousand rust-hued *bhoots,* ghouls wandering the slopes with haunted eyes, groaning under the torment of their captors.

When Harsha met Surpanakha at the slave pen at the end of the day, the sight of her crushed his heart. "Priyatama!" he gasped in horror, catching her as she collapsed into his arms. Blood and sweat streaked the grime that filmed her unclad torso, rivers marking the freshest of her agony.

Her back was the worst he'd seen, torn by countless tiny lashes. "The haraamis mangled you!" He'd never felt so hot a rage, despite the pain in his jaw. "They singled you out! They—"

"Hold me, Harsha." Her voice was a tortured rasp, choked with the fine dust that strangled the entire place.

Harsha was a young man and possessed a wiry strength from years of combat training. Still, he could hardly stand that night as the sun's last light bled out. Muscles large and small shrieked with every move he made; it was agony to simply raise his hand to his mouth to eat his chapati and drink his gruel.

"I wonder if it will always be this way." He sat slouched alongside Surpanakha in their pen, leaning back against the iron bars in a corner, far from the other slaves. Two bands of newcomers had arrived just in the previous four days. Still, the prince and princess were faithfully ignored by the others. Haandi had poisoned the minds of their fellow crew members against them by cutting rations every time the two stumbled.

Stumbling was frequent and tolerated among the slaves, weak as they were. However, Haandi claimed Surpanakha and Harsha never struggled since they were 'fat and sleek as sea dolphins.'

"It's a game," Surpanakha responded weakly. "Just a game, Harsha. Push through, and soon, it will all be over." Blood cracked her lips, beading on the lower curve and dribbling towards her chin as she spoke. Despite the humidity of the nearby wilderness, the heat of the furnaces and the dust of the excavation resulted in an abnormal dryness. Sometimes, it was a torment just to fit their mouths around the tiniest bites of chapati.

But they did not completely lack allies. One tall, haggard woman who looked part Asuran took a particular liking to Surpanakha, offering her a scrap of canvas for protection from the mosquitoes.

"Sly Maragat gave you to Haandi because he's cruel," she sniffed one night. "He's a brute of a man, famous for dividing his slaves, for stoking old hatreds and sparking new ones. It's always the same. Haandi wants to break your spirit, to see the spark of life driven from your eyes. But with you two, it's extra special." She grunted, studying Harsha with weary eyes. "Vidyadhara, you've caused Haandi enough problems already, if what Surpanakha tells me is true. And you even dared insult the commander. Called him a haraami in front of his men? Isn't that 'bastard' in the Vidyadharan tongue?" She chuckled. "Shiva's blood. I wish I'd been there to see that. But he won't forgive you, by Kaala's name. He'll act calm, smile, beat you with little more than a warning, then confidently walk away." Raising a gnarled finger, she tapped her left temple. "But he'll remember, yes. He'll see you bleed for that."

"But they can't treat us like this forever!" Harsha exclaimed. His jaw throbbed every time he spoke. In the short time he'd been there, he saw that newcomers were fed less, sheltered even more poorly, and whipped far more often than the veterans. Still, Surpanakha and he had been given very special attention. "Surely, we're of less use to them the weaker we are!"

"But your spirit!" the woman whispered. "He wants to break your spirit first! You." She jabbed Harsha in the chest. "You walk like a bloody *raajakumara.* Your eyes still flash with fire. You need to bow your head! And you?" It was Surpanakha's turn. She grunted as the woman's nail poked the skin between her breasts. "You're far too beautiful."

"That you are," Harsha muttered, savouring her beauty with his eyes. Surpanakha was bruised, hollow-eyed, and filthy, her hair hanging lank with sweat and grime. Fresh blood caked a swelling on her jaw, and the lash marks on her back were filled with a film of rufous dust.

Her suffering rent his spirit, yet he'd never seen her so beautiful.

A tragic beauty, he thought. *A song of weeping. Of the glorious death of a noble warrior. There is nothing more beautiful nor sadder.* The lines leaped to his mind unbidden, a famous quote from *The Vidyadharan Forging*. It was a play he'd memorized by heart, recited every solstice's eve before roaring throngs of Vidyadharan nobles at the palace of Shaktapur.

Surpanakha is stronger than I will ever be. Every night, he took her in his arms, hidden in the shadows. Their compound was advantageously situated alongside the pens that housed the buffalo. There were several hundred of them penned in the surrounding fields cleared around the mine. They were rotated daily to help in drawing the massive carts that held the ore.

In Harsha's pen, the overpowering odour of the beasts encouraged their crew to huddle in the far end, allowing Harsha and Surpanakha a modicum of privacy if they submitted to the stench. They were largely left alone.

"Your crew's bitterness is a passing thing," Surpanakha's friend muttered. "Their anger is for the pain Haandi brings them, not the happiness that you share. They are not yet so twisted as to confuse the two. A week, and the bitterness towards you will fade."

Her words proved prophetic. The overseers knew an entire crew could not be given short rations for long—production would suffer. Their fellow slaves spoke to them by the sixth day and shared their space by the fire with them on the eighth. While Harsha was an outsider in their largely Asuran and Rakshasan group, he was confident that Surpanakha would slowly win their hearts. So the first time the district overseer came to check on progress, Harsha learned to his pleasure that the Devas had greater Gods to appease than Haandi and his petty anger.

"Priyatama, we need to start winning their hearts and minds," he whispered to Surpanakha. "And then, we'll make our move."

Even though their crew warmed to them, the teens preferred the shadows in the night. Shadows were for comfort and the hidden closeness of each other's bodies.

And for planning. "The opportunity will emerge," Harsha insisted every night, and every night she nodded and said she believed him.

"Harsha, let me heal your jaw with my Asuran magic," said Surpanakha one night as they held each other.

"The pain isn't bad, priyatama, I'll manage."

"Hush! Be quiet and hold your face up." The princess of all Asuras responded as she held his face in her palms and chanted three mantras of healing to Lord Vaitheeswara—Shiva as the celestial physician. Then, with a quick movement, she pushed his jaw up and towards him with some force.

Harsha winced sharply as he pulled back, but slowly, a smile lit up his face as he realized the pain in his jaw had vanished. "You're a miracle worker, Surpanakha!" he exclaimed, pulling her to him.

What a sorry moorkha I am, he thought, closing his eyes and pressing his face to her chest, comforted by the rhythm of her breath. *What a pitiful, hopeless moorkha. So blind, her faith.* It made him cringe in self-loathing every time he promised her freedom.

Blind as it was, it was pure. So pure it gave Harsha the strength he needed to cling to the hope that maybe—perhaps—Shakti would help them escape.

And so, Surpanakha kept them both sane with the artlessness of her blind faith in him.

"At least we still have each other," he whispered thickly one night.

"Yes." She nodded against his chest. "Yes. We still have each other."

* * *

And so it was that the princess of Asurapura and her priyatama, the crown prince of the sapta kula, the seven tribes of the Vidyadharas, came to be enslaved at Ayasapur mine in the heart of the Simha Aranya on Naraka. Will the lovers survive this ordeal? Or perish under the harsh heat and dust of the mine and the backbreaking labour?

What will her brother, the twice-born Asuran sorcerer-prince Ravan do next? Will he bow to the dictates of his mother, Queen Kaikesi of Asurapura, and those of High Priest Shukra? Or penetrate the very depths of the aranya to find his dear sister and the Vidyadharan prince?

These questions and many more are answered in the next book of *The Naraka Cycle*, entitled *Demons and their Gods*, coming soon!

Origins

In the beginning, there was only Potential. *Prakrti.* Power unrealized, Chaos unrealized. Being Itself. Pure Consciousness. All were contained within Her, the womb, the womb of being and of non-being. All that would become, all that would not become. All that would be realized, and all that would not be realized. Pluripotential Possibility. All seeds that would be, that could have been, and that might yet come to germinate—All were within Her. And so Potential Was. There was no Time, no Space, no Causation.

Then, *Prakrti,* Potential, became aware of Herself. Intellect, *Buddhi,* emerged from Her. To become, to be realized, to be given form, to become matter, intellect was born from Her, Intellect distinct from Potential. The intellect that realizes, that intends and brings into being, that orders, and that there might be order, Potential had to separate into two distinct entities. And so the unrealized potential became known as Nature, and the intellect, the spark, became *Purusha.* Three *Purusha* became—*Brahma, Vaishnavi,* and *Shiva,* each with a separate purpose.

From Brahma came Creation, the fashioning of things, the ordering of matter, and potential, into structured actuality. And He was worshipped as the Creator.

From Vaishnavi came Protection of all that is good, the preservation of Brahma's conception, and its perpetuation. And She was deified as the Preserver.

From Shiva came the Destruction of all that is evil and the ending of Brahma's Creation at *pralaya,* the Great Dissolution. And He was bowed to as the Great Destroyer.

And they were known as the *Trimurti.*

In his loneliness, Brahma hummed the primordial sound *Aum.* And from *Aum* emerged the immortal knowledge, the Four Vedas. And so Brahma released from himself four children, children of the mind. The Kumaras he called them—the ancient one, the joyful one, the eternal one, and the ever-young. Without blemish and without guile, they were created, purity incarnate. But still, they were individual, each mind separate and distinct.

And as he had intended, the Lord Brahma commanded them to help him weave creation from their limitation—to fashion bodies of matter and to erect walls between them, and then to breathe mind into the walls, and thus make life.

But the Kumaras refused him. So pure were they, and so consumed by the nature of their not-Father Vaishnavi, that they could not turn their thoughts to any other. To abstinence, they swore, and to eternal youth; and they devoted themselves wholly to wisdom and clarity, the perpetuation of good which they could not see clearly from their Father Brahma's perspective.

Furious, Brahma created more; Limitation—that's what he sought. That there might be entities-creative entities-which were not Him. Which might do things that He would not, which might bring things into realized actuality that He was separate from. This was the only way He could experience change, uncertainty, newness, challenge, beauty—indeed, the only way he could experience.

This time, Ten, he created, and of diverse natures and fabrics, he wove them, strings of many colors into tapestries of person. Manu of morality, Narada of laughter and song, Kratu of procreation, Daksha of skill, Vritra of speed and cunning, Surya of illumination, Shuk Raa of refuge and healing, Brihaspati of strategy, Vikrita of transformation, and Shatarupa of knowledge, they were.

Brahma's children were children not of body but purely mind, great in power, and He bestowed upon them the Breath of Creation, as He alone possessed. And into them, He poured the desire for carnal knowledge, for the joining of flesh and flesh and the seeding of children. And the Prajapatis they were named, nine sons and a single daughter; and Brahma sent them out into the worlds to join him in creation.

Then the Prajapatis created for themselves advisors, the seven Seers. The *Saptarishis* they were. Into the Saptarishis too, the Prajapatis poured the breath of creation so that the Saptarishis wove their own spirit in among the tapestry of beings and of realms. Bharadvaja, Brighu, Gautama, Jamdagni, Kratu, Vashishtha, Vishvamitra, the Seven Seers were, and advisors to their mind-born progenitors, the Prajapatis.

And so, the mind-born Ten went out into their Father's Creation, and they gave it form and life and meaning. And together, they fashioned the vast tapestry of darkness, the space upon which to weave matter into form; and across the tapestry of darkness they wove the stars that burn, and the worlds that spin; and they fashioned the mountains that rise and crumble, and the rivers that flow between them, and the flowers that bloom and wither and the cycling of the rains, the dry, the heat and cold, the light and dark, and death and life of endless turning, *Samsara.*

Realms they created for themselves, and the laws that govern nature *Rta,* all were there, wrought out of the possibility of the Goddess and the intent of their Father.

The Nine and their Sister, Shatarupa, took matter from their bodies and mingled it with *Rta,* laws of Nature, and their Father Brahma's power of Intellect and Creation—what would later become known as magic—and in this way from *Rta* and *Buddhi* gave rise to the realms of the Ten. Then, they scattered wide the realms, letting the waters rush in to fill the spaces in between. And they sowed their seeds, the creatures born of their mind and fire, planting in each realm seeds well suited to it, according to their wisdom. Flesh and blood and bone the Ten made, knitting them with muscle and with sinew, quickening them with breath and thought.

And the Ten divided themselves further, sowing consciousness each according to his design, to his nature, giving thought and will and intent and emotion to beings yet more limited than they—beings which had the urge to create as well but were limited to the laws of each their individual worlds—beings which knew not about the vast overarching scheme of things. And so the beings of flesh and blood possessed morality, laughter, song, skill, speed, cunning, illumination, the will to protect, the need to sacrifice, transform, and learn.

First, Manu created Swarga, a realm of open sky and sunlit grass and rivers through fertile wooded valleys. A frigid winter it had, deep with snow and wandering spirits, but the springs were full of life and water, and the summers lush with growing things.

And joining with his brothers and the Saptarishis, Manu, the Eight, and their Sister created the Devas to live on Swarga, tall, broad-shouldered, strong and swift, with the spark to master the horses that roamed their plains and the winds that scoured their many seas. And on their wondrous creations, the Prajapatis bestowed the primordial mantras of the Four Vedas.

Naraka, of dense aranyas and great peaks, rolling steppes, and red deserts, was formed next under the leadership of Prajapati Shuk Raa. A hot summer, it possessed, and violent monsoons, great snowfall, and parched earth. After their own form, they fashioned the monkeys and migoi apes upright, with hands and feet and inquisitive natures, with eyes two in the front of the head, staring ever forwards, outwards, studying all they came across with cunning eyes and nimble hands and razor minds. In this realm, Vritra the Prajapati created the great serpents. He wove from the serpents of the deep jungle, the vipers cunning, and quick as thought, and constrictors, powerful and ever-patient. He took the poisoned fang of vipers and the dreadful strength of pythons, and he took the heart and spirit of the snake and to it added something more.

Then, Mind, much like their own, the Ten and the Seven gave the serpents, and also their own spirit that bended towards nobility, towards higher learning, spirit that sought to reason, to understand, and finally to control. Narakanform they gave the serpents, upright as the monkeys they'd created, and with eyes both in front of the head, intent and watchful, standing tall to face whatever threatened. But their Serpentform they did not rob from them, instead, giving them the power to change between forms, to move as graceful liquid after the manner of the Prajapatis themselves. Both in the trees and on the land, as serpents and cunning warriors.

Nagas, they were named, and the Prajapatis seeded them across the jungles of Naraka.

From the horses of Swarga, they took form and fashion, the thunder-spirit of the plains and the surging power of the hooves and the endless restless aching for motion, for freedom, for life beneath an open, ever-changing sky. The body of a horse they gave their new creation, but they joined it unto a form like theirs, and like unto the Naga form; the chest and arms and head like they themselves possessed, the Prajapatis. And they made them beautiful and fierce, with faces chiseled hard and strong for war, the men dark lords of terror, singing joyously as they fought; and the women as goddesses who road bare-breasted beneath the rain and smiled ivory teeth dripping crimson with the blood of their enemies.

Kinnaras they were called, scattered across the deserts and the steppes of Naraka, given reign of the open lands where others could not find their path, or would die for want of water, or would quail at the savagery of the thunderstorms that swept the barren vastness of it all.

And they planted more races as beasts, as infants in their realms. And they intended that many ages would pass before the races might advance in wisdom and learning and power, enough to cross the watery expanses which separated them, one realm from another.

And the eons passed, and the children of the Prajapatis went out into the worlds they had sown, and ate of Brahma's fruit and ran upon the realms and drank of the deep waters. And full of life they were, each according to its Song. But no Song is unchanging, no voice unaltered by the melodies that cross its path. And so the creatures mingled, encountering one another; and in encountering one another, each recognized its nature, its rhythm in the shape of things.

And the races of beasts fashioned by the Prajapatis fought in the manner of bounded creatures in a bounded world. They fought and bred and birthed and bled. They grew, and learned, and died. And they began to change.

From the tribes of hunter monkeys on the coastal cliffs, there emerged another strain, stronger, fierce with the spirit of the Prajapatis. Deep of the sea air they breathed and strong in its waters, they began to swim, and they surpassed their brethren in the deeper jungles.

Language they discovered, and tools with which to aid their hunting. And blessed with cunning from Prajapatis Daksha and Vikrita, they built crafts to float upon the water, and nets with which to snare their fish, and spears with which to defend themselves from the larger terrors of the seas.

Rakshasas, they became, a people born of nature which the Prajapatis did not intend. And far they sailed, and boldly; and they charted waters even the Prajapatis knew not, and they faced nearly invincible monsters from the belly of watery abysses that even Brahma seldom saw. Their own tongue they formed, powerful and rolling like the waves. It was a rhythm woven less by the intent of the Prajapatis and more by the slow unfolding of the ages and the scourging wrath of nature. And their sight grew far and free upon the vastness of the open waters, and they learned to read the stars, and chart them, and to know their way by their light, and by every gust of wind, and every ripple of the waters.

And the Prajapatis were awed by the passing of such a thing. So faithful was Brahma's power in them, so potent with cunning and with wisdom were the realms, that the very fabric of creation seemed alive. Not only had they set the stage. Not only had they laid the pieces of the game. No. This was a story that had begun to spin itself, to grow ever beyond the vision of its tellers.

And inspired by these happenings, the Prajapatis ached for more. So from the Rakshasas, they took strength and the watching of stars and the taming of the seas. And with the light and grace of their own forms, they mingled this, returning to their new creation an inward-peering heart that seeks deep knowing, a love of land and stable places, of cunning with words and songs, and of stone cities built over generations.

Asura, they named it, this new wonder of theirs, an echo of matter, mind, and Brahma but also something else, this evolution of the Rakshasa-spirit, this unexpected melody of nature's own design. And Shuk Raa stood alone against the Nine and the Seven to argue that as with the Deva, the Asura, too, ought to receive the primordial knowledge of the Four Vedas.

But Prajapati Shatarupa was not satisfied. She longed to spin from a creature not already awoken to language and to tool. She longed to spin from something still unshaped. Something purer, with wit and will like unto the coastal monkeys, but wilder still. For all the flow of wind and waves, there was too much of iron will, too much of charted memory in Rakshasas.

Shatarupa searched for minds not rigid but beating, pulsing with the mystery of creation. And she saw the migoi, the mighty ice-apes of the north. And drawing from their flesh-code she took eyesight like an eagle's, untiring strength against the cold and the savage joy of battle and the hunt. But she wove with this much of her own figure, her own will, and above all, the wild clarion call of freedom, the laughing joy of challenge, the spark of life that turns to the abyss and leaps, bellowing defiance to the end.

Nature itself, Shatarupa wove. The will to live. And she wove the spark of language on the tongue of her creation, and the spark of inner music that hears Shakti's deepest Song, that which moves in the old and nameless places of the earth.

Music, her brother Narada gave it, but it was not the music of the Asuras, plodding to the rhythms of the mind. This was a music fay and wild, tangled up in the shadows of Nature that stir beyond the knowledge of the waking mind.

Vidyadhara, she and her brothers called it, and the fire in its blood and bones was enough to stand the frigid north. All the scattered peaks she gave their creation, from the northern land bridge to the very threshold of the jungle. And a fierce people they became, and untamed, and beautiful in the way of their wild Peaks, Singers of Nature's very Song.

And as eons passed, the creations of the Prajapatis began to mingle, speak, and learn from one another. And as their knowledge stretched to land, to seas, to skies, they longed for more. So they looked ever onward, in the same spirit of the beings that had given to them life.

And these were but few of the God-formed races.

www.ingramcontent.com/pod-product-compliance
Lightning Source LLC
La Vergne TN
LVHW091314150826
845673LV00006B/1637

* 9 7 9 8 8 8 7 8 3 5 5 0 1 *